Sherri L.

Ride the Lightning

Ellora's Cave
Romantica Publishing

What the critics are saying...

&

"Like every other Sherri L. King book I have ever read, I devoured **Ride the Lightning** the moment I got it. This is one of those books that when you read it, it will make you search for the rest of the series if you haven't read them already. **Ride the Lightning** is a DEFINITE keeper but then again, all of Ms. King's books are."
~*Novelspot*

"...a fast-paced, electric addition to the world of the Shikars. The sex is hot, the Shikar is to-die-for and *Ride The Lightning* is one fabulous read." ~*Joyfully Reviewed*

"...you are in for a delicious and sexed-up treat. Ms. King knows how to titillate the senses and enthrall the mind of her readers with her excellent storytelling."
~*ParaNormal Romance*

"This story is fast paced, interesting, and the sexual chemistry is explosive." ~*TwoLips Reviews*

"Mrs. King has done an excellent job telling the story. If you like paranormal romances that are extra steamy, then this book is one you should definitely read. I will be reading this book again and again in the future."
~*Coffee Time Romance*

An Ellora's Cave Romantica Publication

www.ellorascave.com

Ride the Lightning

ISBN 9781419956331
ALL RIGHTS RESERVED.
Ride the Lightning Copyright © 2006 Sherri L. King
Edited by Kelli Kwiatkowski
Cover art by Darrell King

Electronic book Publication November 2006
Trade paperback Publication May 2007

Excerpt from *Caress of Flame* Copyright © Sherri L. King, 2006

Content Advisory:

S – ENSUOUS
E – ROTIC
X – TREME

Ellora's Cave Publishing offers three levels of Romantica® reading entertainment: S (S-ensuous), E (E-rotic), and X (X-treme).

The following material contains graphic sexual content meant for mature readers. This story has been rated E–rotic.

S-*ensuous* love scenes are explicit and leave nothing to the imagination.

E-*rotic* love scenes are explicit, leave nothing to the imagination, and are high in volume per the overall word count. E-rated titles might contain material that some readers find objectionable—in other words, almost anything goes, sexually. E-rated titles are the most graphic titles we carry in terms of both sexual language and descriptiveness in these works of literature.

X-*treme* titles differ from E-rated titles only in plot premise and storyline execution. Stories designated with the letter X tend to contain difficult or controversial subject matter not for the faint of heart.

Also by Sherri L. King

ༀ

Bachelorette

Beyond Illusion

Ellora's Cavemen: Tales from the Temple III (*anthology*)

Ferocious

Fetish

Manaconda (*anthology*)

Midnight Desires (*anthology*)

Moon Lust 1: Moonlust

Moon Lust 2: Bitten

Moon Lust 3: Mating Season

Moon Lust 4: Feral Heat

Rayven's Awakening

Sanctuary

Caress of Flame

Sin and Salvation

Sterling Files 1: Steele

Sterling Files 2: Vicious

Sterling Files 3: Fyre

Sterling Files 4: Hyde

The Horde Wars 1: Ravenous

The Horde Wars 2: Wanton Fire

The Horde Wars 3: Razors Edge

The Horde Wars 5: Lord of the Deep

The Jewel

Full Moon Xmas

About the Author

ଌ

Sherri L. King lives in the American Deep South with her husband, artist and illustrator Darrell King. Critically acclaimed author of The Horde Wars and Moon Lust series, her primary interests lie in the world of action packed paranormals, though she's been known to dabble in several other genres as time permits.

Sherri welcomes comments from readers. You can find her website and email address on her author bio page at www.ellorascave.com.

Tell Us What You Think

We appreciate hearing reader opinions about our books. You can email us at Comments@EllorasCave.com.

RIDE THE LIGHTNING

⁊ↄ

Dedication

ஐ

For D.

Trademarks Acknowledgement

ஐ

The author acknowledges the trademarked status and trademark owners of the following wordmarks mentioned in this work of fiction:

BMW: Bayerische Motoren Werke Aktiengesellschaft

Cartoon Network: The Cartoon Network LP, LLLP

Chevy Impala: General Motors Corporation

Coke: The Coca-Cola Company

Glock: Glock, Inc.

Godiva: Godiva Brands, Inc.

Hilton: Hilton Hospitality, Inc.

Powerball: Multi-State Lottery Association

Prologue

ॐ

"Are you sure you want to do this? You haven't explored the surface in many decades. A lot has changed in that time. More than you know," Flare said, glancing at him with some concern.

"That is precisely why I am going. It has been far too long since I truly explored the Territories," Pulse explained patiently. "I wish to once again look upon the world and remember why we battle so hard to keep the Earth and its people safe."

Flare sighed wearily. "Does this have anything to do with the night we went to Isis' family home?"

Pulse sighed heavily. "Partly," he admitted. "That night I saw how evil and malicious humans can be towards each other. It has, I fear, made me see humans in a different light—one that I know isn't fair to all. I need to be reminded that not all humans are like that. That the world of the human race is truly worth saving."

"How long will you visit up there amongst the humans?" Flare asked curiously.

"As long as I have to." Pulse packed the last of his clothing in the ancient steamer trunk and closed it with a snap. "I have already informed the Council of my decision and they have agreed that my intentions are just. If there are any emergencies here, I will of course come back at once. But I know the Council can take care of itself and our people. I have no worries that my absence will cause any strife for anyone."

"I will visit often to receive your orders and—"

"To check up on me," Pulse broke in, smiling patiently. "You needn't worry so, Flare. I am more than capable of taking care of myself."

Flare bowed his head respectfully. "I know you speak the truth, Generator, and I am sorry if I offended you."

Pulse took the handle of the trunk and swung it off the bed. "You know you have not offended me. But I can see right through you. You feel a responsibility towards me. That is as it should be. Though I am your superior, I am also your comrade in arms. We have fought together, bled together and we have a bond that will not be easily shaken. Rest assured, I know you have the best of intentions. But please believe me when I tell you that I will be safe enough on the surface. I have done this before with no trouble."

"But civilization has raced forward in the years since you spent any great amount of time in the Territories. Things are very different now than they were even ten years ago, let alone…what? Fifty, sixty years ago?"

Pulse placed a hand on Flare's shoulder. "I command you not to worry about me. I will adapt—it is what we are all good at."

Flare knew better than to argue further. "I shall look forward to your return."

"You have your orders. Patrol the Territories, look for Daemon activity. I know you well, Flare. I am confident that you will not fail in your duties. I have the utmost faith in you."

Flare nodded and clasped his hand on Pulse's shoulder in return. "Be well, my Elder."

Pulse smiled and his stern features transformed into a handsome beauty. "I will. And you as well, my friend."

* * * * *

Much *had* changed since last he'd been in the Territories—that was plain the moment Pulse arrived in New York City. For one, there were thousands more people than he expected. There was more pollution choking the air, more loud noises that shrieked in his ears and grated on his nerves, more unrest and antagonism amongst the humans, as if they didn't trust one another at all. No one made eye contact with him. He needn't have worn the brown contacts to hide his Shikar eyes after all—no one would have noticed his real eyes anyway.

Upon his arrival he went to a hotel, one well lit and with the rooms on the inside. He checked into a suite, astonished at how costly it was to stay even one night. But it didn't matter. He had endless funds and could well afford it. Still...he was no fool. Money was important in this world, and it seemed one must have much of it to experience any sort of creature comfort.

He was disappointed to see how small the room was when he reached it. Pulse was used to wide-open spaces. Lots and lots of space. But this city was so heavily populated he knew he shouldn't be surprised that they valued their space like a rich commodity. The room would do. He surmised that he probably wouldn't be spending much time there anyway.

Pulse put away his things in the small wardrobe that was provided. There was an odd box on top of the dresser that faced the bed. He studied it carefully and pressed the button labeled "power". The box flared to life, startling him with the sheer volume of sound coming from what seemed to be deceptively tiny speakers.

He found the wand on top of the box without really knowing what it was—it was covered in colorful buttons with captions that meant nothing to him. It was just a bunch of numbers and buttons labeled "channel" and "volume" and "menu". He didn't understand how it worked. Pulse simply pressed buttons until the pictures on the box changed and then changed again. At last, with a disgusted grunt, he put the wand down and turned the box off.

The lights were bright in the room. Too bright for comfort. He wandered around the room and turned some of them off—the switches he understood from his last visit to the surface world—and the room dimmed to a more pleasant glow, one that he could more easily see in.

Pulse went to his window and pushed open the heavy drapes that would protect him from the bright rays of the sun. There was a latch on the window, allowing him to open it a sliver. But only a sliver. He couldn't understand why humans wouldn't want to invite more fresh air into their quarters...then he heard the noises of the people and machines below.

He had a good view of the city up here on the sixth floor. Lights were everywhere—in the buildings, on the streets, on enormous advertisement boards. Everywhere. Hundreds of cars traveled the black roads, their honking horns loud, even among the din of too many people in one place at the same time. The air smelled heavily of smoke and refuse. The scents were vile—nearly as bad as Europe more than a century ago. Pulse had no idea how the humans could function without suffering major mental and physical health issues because of all the madness.

Entranced, he watched the ebb and flow of traffic beneath his window. Indeed, much had changed since he'd been here over half a century ago. He would have to learn the city all over again, and he knew for certain that it would not be easy to acclimate to such an alien environment. He needed to learn much if he was to survive for any length of time here in the Territories of Earth.

Pulse was eager to get started. He turned away from the window and left the room without a backward glance.

Chapter One

೮೨

Luna Boone was waiting for a tragedy to happen.

In her twenty-four years of life she had seen much—
and not all of it was pretty. She was used to seeing the very
worst side of human nature, the bestial creatures all
humans were deep down inside. More than most, she knew
that beneath the sliver of our higher brains lies a reptilian
brain that wants nothing more than to fight and maim.
Luna accepted this, yet still she was hopeful that she could
change things.

Her hopefulness was naturally sometimes shaken by
despair. But she refused to become weak and despondent,
as her mother had been. The road to weakness led only to
madness, and she just wasn't ready to give up control of her
resolve quite yet.

The world was a dark and dangerous place with many
hidden secrets and twisted desires. Luna had been taught
that since the cradle and she truly believed it some of the
time. But she *wanted* to believe otherwise. Desperately. She
wanted to see the beauty and innocence in the world. She
knew it must be there somewhere—and she *would* find it, if
only she searched hard enough.

Will I be strong enough to see this through? she wondered.
Would this be the time that she finally changed things? Her
brain itched with questions and none of them had answers,
at least none that Luna could see. She would simply have to
wait and watch and find out. She glanced at her watch for
what must have been the hundredth time since arriving on
the street corner in front of the Times Square Hilton.

Fifteen minutes left.

Luna didn't know how she was going to prevent it from happening. She'd never before succeeded in changing the outcome of her predictions, only little pieces of them that seemed to have no real effect on the end result. Still, she had to try. She was the only one who knew it would happen and thus it was her responsibility to try and change things. It was her gift and her curse and she must do her part, whatever that was.

For many years she'd done her best to prevent the premonitions from coming true, but it had been a fruitless endeavor. Fate, it seemed, was already written and Luna had no idea how to rewrite it. Yet there was still a desperate need in her to *try*. This, too, was part of her curse.

It wouldn't be easy, fighting to prevent the tragedy. But she would persevere and hold fast to her courage despite the odds, despite the near certainty that she would fail. She always did, even if it didn't do anyone else any good.

Out of the corner of her eye she saw a black shape exit the hotel. Why this shadow caught her attention, turning it away from her true mission, she couldn't have said. But the man in black was something she'd never encountered before. She almost couldn't believe her eyes.

He was handsome as all get-out—that, of course, caught her attention first. The black hair on his head was long, down to the middle of his back and unbound. The wind teased the strands and tiny streaks of silver glinted in the lights. The exotic vision of it held her mesmerized for precious seconds when she should have been thinking on what was about to happen.

Yet still Luna couldn't help watching him. He was dressed strangely, in a soft, loose-fitting tunic and equally soft-looking pants, but the style was foreign, like none she was familiar with. He had boots on his feet, shiny and black with tarnished silver buckles that did nothing to disguise how big his feet were. In fact, all of him was big, she realized. He had to stand just a few inches below seven feet. Luna had never seen someone as tall as he in person, only on televised basketball games. He presented quite an imposing figure of masculine strength.

His shoulders were shockingly broad and undoubtedly strong. He had a handsome face, a surprisingly square jaw and a long, strong nose. Smooth, unblemished skin the rich color of bronze indicated he was definitely not Caucasian, or at least if he was it was mixed with something else more exotic. His midnight-dark brows flared artfully over his brown eyes and—

His eyes weren't brown. She knew it—suddenly and with a familiar certainty.

Curious, she watched as a vagrant approached the man, begging for money. She felt her eyes bulge when the man quite unexpectedly handed the vagrant a thick wad of bills. The vagrant nearly fainted, blubbering his thanks before swiftly departing, no doubt fearing the dark stranger would change his mind and take the money back.

Luna approached the odd stranger as if magnetically drawn to him, leaving her post by the bustling street—something she would never, ever have done before. She couldn't help herself—her instincts were practically singing an aria and she could do no less than indulge her curiosity.

"He's going to spend that on booze, you know. He'll be dead in two months from alcohol poisoning," she told him by way of greeting.

The man glanced down at her as if he'd never seen another human being before and she instinctively took a step back. There was an arrogance and disdain in his eyes that Luna didn't like one bit. He looked as if he owned the world, and the people in it were only living there because he allowed them to.

Feeling a thrill of that "other" awareness that was so much a part of her, she glanced at her watch, tearing her eyes away from his artificially colored ones with great effort. Ten minutes to go.

Despite the urgency driving her, Luna eyed him once more, her gaze drawn to him as if by a force greater than her will. She wondered just what it was about him that had caught her attention. It was true that he was probably the best-looking man she'd ever seen, but it was more than that, and Luna had long ago learned to trust her instincts. And right now her instincts demanded she pay attention to this stranger.

A figurative light dawned in her mind and she gasped softly in surprise before she could swallow the revealing sound. The man had looked away from her during the few seconds of her revelation, taking in his surroundings like a thirsty sponge. And it was no wonder. Luna doubted he'd been on Earth for very long.

"You're not human," she said, knowing it was a fact and unafraid to say so...though perhaps it wasn't the wisest thing to do. This man looked—and felt—very, very dangerous.

Her proclamation drew his attention immediately. His gaze met hers and she nodded her certainty, determined to meet his intense countenance, despite her common sense. "That's right, I said it...you're not human. So, uh...what are you then?" she dared to ask, practically dancing in her eagerness to hear his answer, if he would dare to speak.

The man approached her gracefully, as if his feet floated above the ground, dwarfing her in his shadow, large body moving in a way that was keenly predatory. His scent reached her nose—fragrant, like the forest after a rain.

It tickled her nose and teased all her other senses until she reeled drunkenly.

In shock, Luna watched, her mind detached from the moment as if she suffered from some unknown spell, as he reached out and put his hands on either side of her face. The touch of his skin on hers sent a jolt through her body, as if she'd been shocked by a staggering bolt of electricity. She'd never experienced such a powerful reaction to anyone before, man or woman, and though it probably should have scared her, and might have on a normal night, she felt no fear.

"You will forget you saw me," he said quietly, firmly, his tone a command, pure and simple.

Shaking off her fugue with supreme effort, Luna tugged his hands away, knowing instinctively what he was trying to do, though how she knew she couldn't say. A nervous giggle escaped and she slapped her hand over her mouth before collecting herself. "That won't work on me," she said, knowing it was true just as she knew so many things that others might never believe or understand. He had been trying to tamper with her memory. It would have been almost comical if the man didn't look so dangerous. She might have laughed outright if she hadn't been so shocked at what he'd so casually tried to do—what he'd fully and confidently believed he *could* do.

"Who are you?" the man asked with a slight frown that only served to make him more handsome. There was great curiosity in his tone, and really, she couldn't blame him.

What a weird night.

"I'm Luna. Who are *you*?" She felt her lips stretch into a grin and her heartbeat pick up its tempo.

"I am Pulse."

Now she did laugh, softly. "Great. At least we know we share one thing in common. We both have weird names." Her attempt at humor did not elicit a response from Pulse, who merely looked at her from his great height, his eyes roving over her face and form as if she were a lab specimen and he was trying to figure out what species she belonged to.

Pulse turned to go without a word. Luna scowled at his rudeness, not a little disappointed at his dismissal. She grabbed his sleeve and halted him. "Please. What are you?" She had to know.

"I am a Shikar," he answered shortly, before once again turning away from her completely.

Luna had never heard the word before. "Are you an alien?" she asked, relentless in her curiosity.

He turned once more to face her and she felt a strange current in the air, and the hairs on her body stood on end.

"No."

His answer was short and curt, telling her plainly without additional words that he wanted her gone from him.

Luna ignored his surly attitude. "Why are you here?" She compulsively glanced at her watch and saw that precious minutes were ticking away. It wouldn't be much longer and no matter how fascinating the past few moments had been, she was here for a much higher purpose, one that could not wait. "Hang on a sec," she continued hurriedly as an idea began to coalesce in her mind. "It doesn't matter what you are. But I think I could really use your help."

The man looked instantly concerned, an entire reversal from his previous attitude, his emotions written plainly on his face for her to read. She rather liked that.

"How may I aid you?" he asked formally.

Luna swallowed hard. She hadn't told many people about her strange power, but she thought this man just might believe her story, where others would think her mad. "There's going to be an accident in five minutes," she said quickly and without preamble. "Right there." She pointed to the street beyond the sidewalk they stood on. "A car is going to flip and a woman is going to be hurt, trapped inside it, upside down. I'll only have one and a half minutes to get her out of the car before a bus comes by and obliterates it, killing her instantly."

Pulse frowned and his artificially dark eyes searched her own. Within the depths of his gaze she could see the power of his curiosity and, dare she hope, belief. "How do you know this?"

"Um…" She trailed off, trying to think of a good way to explain that which she herself didn't really understand. "Have you ever heard of Cassandra Syndrome? Wait, scratch that. Let me just explain by saying that I have this habit of knowing things before they happen."

She didn't add that she only knew when *tragic* events were going to occur, not good or positive ones. Her power just didn't work that way. It would have been far more useful if she could predict the lottery numbers or know when a gentle rain was going to come. But she never knew things like that. Only bad things. Sometimes *really* bad things. And like the Cassandra of Greek myth…well, there wasn't much hope of things turning out all right no matter what she did.

"I could really use your help," she persisted. "You look strong and I'll need that strength to get the woman— Candy—out of her car." The woman's name had come to her at once, like a light turning on in her brain. She wasn't surprised. This was usually how her curse worked.

22

Pulse regarded her for a long, silent moment while Luna worried over the passage of seconds. "I will aid you in any way I can," he finally told her, quietly, firmly.

For reasons Luna couldn't explain, even to herself, she knew she could trust this man to be true to his word.

Luna looked at her watch again. "Three more minutes," she told him. "Come on, let's get closer to the road." She reached for his hand but he pulled back, as if not wanting to touch her again, and she let her own drop. She turned and walked back to her post by the street, trying not to feel the sting of his rejection.

Pulse followed her to the edge of the sidewalk and waited silently at her side. "Why do you wish to save her?" he asked at last, as if truly interested in her response.

"Because I have to," she said simply. It was the only real truth she knew.

"Do you know this woman?" He cocked his head to the side in a nearly adorable expression of perplexed curiosity. Well, it would have been adorable if he didn't look so sinisterly dangerous.

"No," she answered truthfully, hoping he wouldn't think her crazy, turn tail and run before she could engage his aid. "Never met her."

"But you know she will be hurt." One dark, sculpted eyebrow rose dubiously.

It wasn't really a question. Luna was glad that, at least for the moment, he seemed willing to believe what she claimed the next few moments would bring.

"Yeah. And I really don't want that to happen. You see, she's pregnant too, and the baby will die along with her if I can't stop this from happening." Luna neglected to tell him that she'd never before been able to stop a vision from coming true. She'd been able to change some aspects of the premonitions, true, but ultimately the outcome was always far beyond her means to control.

Pulse nodded, his gaze on hers. "We will save her," he said confidently.

Luna could almost believe him, he sounded that sure of himself. But in her heart she knew better. Still, there was always that spark of hope burning deep inside her.

Without looking left or right, Luna abruptly stepped out into traffic, holding her hands out at her sides like a scarecrow. A cab slammed on its brakes and very nearly hit her before coming to a halt but a few short inches away. Luna looked back at Pulse, who was regarding her as if she were a crazy person. She couldn't blame him. "We need this cab here to keep her from skidding too far and hitting another car," she explained with a wry grin as the driver of the cab screamed obscenities at her.

Just then the sound of squealing tires on asphalt caught their attention and they both watched in fascinated horror as a little red BMW lost control in a parallel lane and slid, turning sideways and flipping twice before coming to rest upside down in the middle of the busy roadway, bumping jarringly into the bumper of the cab.

The driver of the cab nearly fell out of his car in his rush to flee.

Never hesitating, Luna ran to the demolished car. Pulse was hot on her heels without any instruction from her and Luna was more than grateful. When they reached the driver's side Luna could clearly see the unconscious driver, still held captive by her seat belt, and her heart lurched.

Luna reached for her but Pulse shoved her gently aside. Luna landed on her backside with a grunt and watched as Pulse took control of the situation, as if he were used to assuming command of any and every aspect of other people's lives. He swiftly delved into the mangled wreck and yanked on the seat belt holding the woman captive with an easy and surprising strength. The belt broke, the metal buckle flying wildly, and Candy fell down into his waiting arms, limp and lifeless.

Luna looked up and saw the bus, still a couple blocks away but coming at them. "Hurry," she urged her strange friend, feeling the press of time like a weight on her soul.

Pulse effortlessly pulled Candy from her car and gently carried her back to the sidewalk. He laid her down carefully on the ground and looked to Luna for what to do next.

Damned if she herself knew what to do. This was the closest she'd ever come to changing the future, and to say that this was alien territory for her would be a great understatement.

Tires screamed, capturing their attention once again. The dreaded bus came barreling down the street, far too fast even in the thick traffic, and Luna knew it was due to the alcohol content in the bus driver's bloodstream. Seeing the danger, the driver slammed on his brakes in an effort to halt his massive vehicle but the bus couldn't stop in time, it was simply moving too fast, with too much mass behind it, and the laws of physics could not be ignored. It hit the BMW with a deafening crash, obliterating the smaller vehicle to nothing more than broken metal and scattered parts that flew like shrapnel around the busy road.

By now, of course, a number of people had gathered to watch the spectacle. They'd seen the first accident, seen both Luna and Pulse go to the driver's aid. Even more spectators had approached to watch, mesmerized, as the bus hit the BMW, came to a screeching halt and skidded several feet before it finally stopped. Two more cars behind it slammed into the rear of the bus and the night air was filled with the sound of crushing metal and squealing tires.

Pulse put his hand on Candy's head, as gently as he might have touched a child. He looked up at Luna who watched them both intently, stunned that for the first time her premonition had somehow been altered from its predestined course.

"She's unconscious, but there is no damage save for a few bruises and scrapes," he told her, and Luna's heart literally stopped for a couple of uncomprehending seconds.

How could he know that? And what did it matter that he did? She quelled the shock that threatened to overwhelm her. "What about her baby?" Luna managed at last, worrying her bottom lip. "Can you tell if her baby is going to be okay?"

Pulse nodded, lightly caressing the swell of Candy's stomach. "It is well."

Luna felt the most blessed relief flood through her and reeled as the blood rushed painfully to her head. "Thank you! Thank you *so much* for your help, Pulse," she said with heartfelt appreciation. "I…I don't know what…I can't believe this happened! Without you… Thank you so much," she said again, at a loss for words to express her deep emotion, laughing and crying at the same time.

An ambulance arrived with much fanfare and the EMTs swiftly surveyed the scene. They spotted Candy's still form and shoved their way through the crowd to reach her. Luna and Pulse both stepped back and let the EMTs do their jobs. Minutes later, they carted the woman away on a stretcher.

Luna had never felt such intense, sweet relief in her entire life.

Other emergency vehicles had come screaming down the street by now. Pulse winced and Luna caught his look before he hid it behind a blank mask. She supposed the loud wails of the sirens hurt his ears. They certainly hurt *hers*.

The events of the past few minutes crowded her mind. Never in her life had she changed the outcome of one of her predictions. And she owed it all to this strange...well, she supposed she couldn't call him a man. A Shikar, then—isn't that what he'd called himself? She thought so, though the word was strange and foreign to her. Anyway, Pulse had helped her when so few would have even *believed* her story, and he had saved Candy and her unborn child from certain death. Luna knew there was no way she could ever explain to him the enormity of the good he had done.

Luna snapped out of her reverie, looked around and saw with shocked dismay that Pulse had already walked half a block away from the din. She ran to follow him, catching up and grabbing his sleeve to slow his long strides, careful lest she touch his skin and experience that strange shock. "Where are you going?" she asked, reluctant to say goodbye so soon to this fascinating stranger.

Pulse looked down at her haughtily. "What business is it of yours?" His tone was deep and hard as the crust of the Earth.

Luna didn't mind his grumpy attitude. Heck, nothing could have ruined her good mood just now. Besides, she knew he didn't mean to hurt her feelings. Well...it *seemed* that he didn't. "None," she answered with a short grin. "But I still want to know. How long have you been here?"

"I arrived tonight," he answered with a great show of patience. "And I am now going to...sightsee."

"Are you here to infiltrate our gene pool?"

Pulse looked shocked for a moment then he laughed. He looked as if he didn't laugh often enough and Luna enjoyed the sound of his mirth. "No," he said at last, catching his breath. "I'm just here to watch and learn."

"Are you planning an alien takeover?" She knew she'd seen too many science-fiction movies but she still couldn't help asking. They were walking again now, Luna struggling to keep up with his giant strides. His legs were so *long*!

"I am *not* an alien," he reiterated with a roll of his eyes.

"Then please, don't keep me in suspense any longer. What are you and why are you really here?" Luna pressed.

Pulse stopped and she tripped to a stop beside him. It was darker here, away from the lights of Times Square, and shadows played about his face, preventing her from seeing his expression. She hated not being able to read a person's face, and she knew instinctively that in order to understand this strange being she would need every advantage she could get.

"You wish to know what I am?"

"Yes," she said eagerly, clasping her hands compulsively together. Squeeze and release, squeeze and release.

A strange glow penetrated his dark contacts and a frisson of sexual awareness danced along her nerves. So potent, so delicious, she reveled in the unusual sensations racing through her blood. It became difficult to concentrate on his response. "I will tell you. But you must first promise me that you will never again step out into traffic the way you did tonight."

Surprised at the direction of his concern, Luna shrugged, wondering at what she viewed as a most strange request. "Sure."

"You promise?"

A bark of laughter made her lips tickle. "Yeah, I promise. Now tell," she pressed impatiently.

Pulse took a deep breath. "I am from a warrior race that lives deep in the Earth's crust. We have been waging a silent battle for many centuries. We protect the innocent from a great evil that threatens to take over the land. We keep humans safe from monsters that want nothing more than to wreak havoc and cause suffering. I am here because I have recently seen how black human hearts can be, and I need to remind myself why we fight so hard to protect such a self-destructive race. Does that explanation satisfy your curiosity?" he asked with a surly frown.

Luna felt shocked to her toes. "You said you fight monsters?"

"Yes. Daemons."

Holy jumping Jesus on a pogo stick! she thought. Was this really happening or had she gone crazy at last?

Taking a deep breath she went with her instincts, as was her nature. "Uh, I'll bet I know the monsters you're talking about," she told him hurriedly. "I've seen them more than a few times, when I was younger, but I haven't seen them in years. They're worse than horrible—they're nightmarish. And they're very difficult to kill. Am I close to what you're referring to?"

It was Pulse's turn to look shocked. Luna knew it was not an expression he was used to wearing. "You have actually *seen* a Daemon? With your own eyes?"

She nodded emphatically. "Absolutely. Before I left home I saw them pretty often. I've killed one of them—my mom showed me how, but it wasn't easy. You have to...I don't know...stop their hearts from beating or something to keep them from getting up again and again. That took me a while to learn. I made a lot of mistakes the first few times I tried to kill the bastards, let me tell you, even with Mom's help." She shuddered with revulsion.

"You have fought these Daemons?"

His gaze swept over her from head to toe, as if he couldn't quite believe her words. And she couldn't blame him. She didn't exactly look like a monster killer. She was only five feet tall, for Christ's sake. But she was determined and she was smart, and the Daemons were—for the most part—quite stupid. Luna had learned early that their greatest weakness was strategy and she had eagerly used that to her advantage.

"Yeah," she admitted, shrugging casually. "And I'm sure I'll fight a few more before it's all over with. They like to show up at the most inopportune times."

"Before what's over with?" he asked, ignoring her last words.

"My life," she said with a quirk of her lips. "I'm going to die pretty soon."

Pulse was dumbfounded. "You know this?"

"Well, yeah. It's a fact," she said with a nod of her head. "Everyone dies eventually. But I'm going to freeze to death during a blizzard or something. That part isn't too clear, but I know for sure that I'll freeze to death. Probably pretty soon."

"You can't know that," he said stonily, as if demanding that she take the words back.

She chuckled mirthlessly and rubbed her hand against her perspiring forehead. "Yes, I can. I do." She didn't like talking about this.

"How can you know these things and not be driven mad by them?" he asked her, shocked.

Luna frowned, puzzled at his sudden concern, and shrugged. She'd long ago accepted her curse and all the trappings that came with it. She didn't like them, but she was wise enough to know she couldn't change them. "I know a lot of things. It's always been a part of who I am, to see things before they happen. For instance," she pointed down the street, "there's a man hanging around over there who's killed two women—prostitutes who no one has noticed missing except a couple beat cops. He's going to kill another woman tomorrow night and his success at avoiding detection will make him cocky. He'll leave a semen sample at the scene. He's been in trouble with the law before for rape, and his DNA is on file. The police will arrest him three days from now."

Pulse gaped at her.

"It's true," Luna said as convincingly as she could.

"We must stop him from killing his next victim," he insisted heatedly, as if there was no other choice.

Amateurs.

"If we try to stop him, he won't be caught," she explained patiently.

"Then let our own justice be swift upon him. We will ensure that he never harms another woman again."

"Look, I know you want to help. But it won't matter. Before tonight, I've never been able to change the outcome of a premonition. If you hadn't been here to help, I don't think I would have been able to save that woman at all. One can't normally change fate."

"But perhaps *two* can," he said with an enigmatic look on his handsome face. "Perhaps, together, we can stop this horrible crime from happening."

Luna thought for a moment and chose her next words carefully. "We can try. But I am almost certain that our efforts will be for nothing. Can you live with that when it happens? Most people couldn't."

"We have to try," he said firmly, determinedly.

"All right. We'll do things your way and see what happens." She nodded reluctantly. "After all, you *did* change fate tonight. Maybe you can do it again." A small spring of hope welled within her...and hope, she knew, could be a dangerous and heartrending thing. Still, she rather liked hope.

"*We* did it. Together," he replied, his tone brooking no argument.

Luna let his words sink in and she felt a spurt of pride that she had, indeed, helped to save that woman and her baby from certain death.

"Do you know where he will strike?" Pulse asked, jolting her out of her introspection.

"Yeah. Not far from Chinatown," she answered easily, glad to have that little bit of information.

"Can you lead me there?" he asked. Now he was the relentless one.

Luna nodded slowly. "Sure. If you really want me to."

"I do."

"Cool." She held out her hand to shake his. Pulse stared down at her hand as if he didn't know what to do with it. Luna realized with a start that he probably *didn't*.

She reached for his hand and shook it. "This seals our deal," she told him. "So I guess I'll meet you outside your hotel again tomorrow night. Let's say eight o'clock. That will give us an hour to stop...John." The name came to her like a bubble of thought deep within her mind. "An hour should be enough time. Perhaps we can pull it off."

"We can," Pulse said arrogantly.

Luna laughed, feeling far more lighthearted than she had in years. "I'll see you tomorrow night then."

She tore her hand away from his and turned to leave. Then, on impulse, she turned and quickly embraced him. Her head barely reached his heart. "Thank you," she said softly into the strange material of his tunic. "Thank you so much for what you did."

He hesitated to put his arms around her, but Pulse knew she hadn't seen the sudden flare of desire in his artificially colored eyes. And she certainly didn't feel the instant erection her embrace gave him. Pulse felt most certain of the last—he didn't think she would have responded well to such a reaction. Humans, he knew from experience, needed time to adjust to desire and passion, while Shikars reveled in it, needing only a short time to know if they wanted another.

And he did want this woman, he realized at once.

Badly.

How could he not? She was the most interesting creature he'd ever encountered—and that was a monumental thing, to say the very least.

It was only a matter of time before they joined. He didn't have to be psychic to know that.

Luna released him, gave him one last beautiful smile that wrenched his heart in a way he'd never experienced, and walked away. He watched her go until she disappeared from sight, eyes drinking in the sight of her round, swaying bottom. And he wondered what the hell he had just gotten himself into.

For better or worse, he knew that Luna's future was fully entwined with his. And he found himself eager to see her again.

Chapter Two

ഇ

Luna lived out of her car. She had for the past year.

She had a little money, thanks to her mom's frugal hoarding of cash, but she didn't feel the need to use it on a home or place to stay. Luna was used to being on the road, driving from city to city, racing to escape her past and ignoring what she knew would happen to her in the future. She liked being mobile.

Sometimes, when she reached a new city, her premonitions would cease for several blessed, wonderful weeks. Eventually, of course, they always came back, but those few weeks of peace were what kept her going. She slept through most days, liking the night far better than the day. In the sunlight everything looked harsh and dirty to her. But in the dark, well...Luna could ignore the suffering and poverty happening all around her.

Mostly.

It was difficult for her to keep a job. Her life was just too complicated for that. It was nearly impossible to hide her gifts around people who were familiar with her and she'd learned early on to keep her relationships with others brief and unemotional. People naturally feared what they didn't understand and she didn't like knowing that she could, without intent or warning, strike fear into the minds and hearts of others.

Inevitably, when she was a bit younger, Luna had tried to put her powers to good use. She had approached the local law enforcement and told them about a horrible crime that was about to be committed. The police hadn't believed her and the crime, of course, had occurred. She'd even been held as a suspect for several days. Once she'd been cleared of the crime, she hit the road and never looked back. Luna had learned valuable lessons during that difficult time.

One was that the Cassandra curse her mother had preached to her since the cradle was a very real one.

Another was that no one wanted to know the future. Even if that knowledge meant the difference between life and death.

And she couldn't blame them. *She* certainly didn't want to know the future. But, sadly, she didn't have control over that. Knowing events that had yet to happen had been her gift—her curse—since puberty, just as it had been her mother's before her and so on and so on ad infinitum.

Luna knew many in her position would be despondent. And sometimes she did feel despair. But Luna had learned early to appreciate life for its own sake. And knowing when and how one would die made one appreciate life all the more. Each and every day was a gift, she knew, and she met them with joy and thanks in her heart.

And today, waking early enough to see the brilliant sunset over the smoggy horizon, she had even more reason to be thankful. Last night she had been able to help prevent one of her premonitions from happening—with a little help, of course. Until last night, Luna had thought such a thing was just simply impossible, even though she'd tried dozens of times and knew she would keep on trying until her life ended. She had believed, before last night, that fate was set in stone and no mere mortal could change it.

But it wasn't. Fate could provide for more than one inevitable outcome. Luna couldn't wait to meet up with her strange new friend again and try to prevent the murder she felt sure would happen tonight. She wanted to see if fate could be changed again. Perhaps alone, as a sufferer of the Cassandra Syndrome, she was powerless, but Pulse had proved to her that, with his help, she wasn't completely without control, and this brought such solace to her heart it was almost bittersweet.

Pulse had occupied her thoughts since they'd parted. It was as if she could think of nothing else. She went over and over in her mind the events of the previous night. She remembered how strong and sure Pulse had been, how caring for the injured Candy, and how determined he had been to stop tonight's crime. She remembered his surliness but she also remembered his gentleness, and knew that he was a good man...Shikar. Whatever.

He was so different from any man she'd ever known that he fascinated her completely. It wasn't just that he was handsome — and he most definitely was that — and it wasn't because he wasn't human, either. Which, by itself, was totally cool. Instead, it was his easy strength and confidence that caught her interest and held it. He cared about humans, even if he *was* currently looking for proof that not all humans were evil. He felt it was his sworn duty to protect humans — that was plain to see in his proud face and expressive eyes and in nearly every word he spoke. It was evident that he was loyal as well as courageous, and arrogantly confident.

Luna had known from the first that he was not human, of course. She didn't know how, but she didn't question it. There was no point. And when she'd confronted Pulse he hadn't denied her allegations. True, he had tried to mess with her head a little bit, tamper with her memory or whatever, but he'd failed and moved on, telling her about his race with little hesitation. She couldn't wait to find out more about him.

The events that were destined to happen tonight were gruesome and Luna hoped she could persevere long enough to make a difference in the very probable outcome. She'd never tried to stop so heinous a crime, not since going to the police a few years before. It would be dangerous in the extreme and she would be lying to herself if she didn't admit that she was more than a little nervous about it.

But Luna wasn't afraid. With a man—*Shikar*—like Pulse at her side, how could she be? Besides, she knew how she was going to die and it wasn't by the hand of a serial murderer. She had little to worry about.

Still, she would take her fire axe. She kept the weapon in the back of her car for emergencies. She'd never bought a gun...she was actually afraid of them. But the axe had come in handy during the past and Luna had a strong feeling that the axe would come in handy at a very crucial moment tonight.

Luna left her car in the ride-share parking lot where she slept and, taking a change of clothing with her, walked to a nearby deli. Once there, she bought a ham sandwich on wheat with lettuce and mayonnaise. The first bite was delicious, the second even more so, and Luna ate her meal swiftly and with gusto, feeling the energy of the food fill her physical form. She was sitting outside under the deli's awning, in a cramped space that was meant to be cozy, but she didn't like feeling hemmed in so she hurried, eating the last few bites of her meal without tarrying. When she was finished, she drank her soda and left the deli, walking down the street and into the heart of the city.

There was a large truck stop not far from the deli with working showers inside. Luna stopped there as she did every night and bathed herself, shedding the worries of the previous day as she shed her dead layers of skin. After washing her hair, long and thick and pale blonde, she braided it tightly in the hopes that no one would pull it in the struggle that lay ahead.

That done, she dressed in fresh clothing and left the truck stop, walking several blocks to a street where little independent shops lined the road. She found a man selling flowers on the street and she bought a bouquet of daisies for two dollars. Holding them close, sad that the flowers would fade in only a few hours but grateful for their last lingering vestiges of beauty, she continued walking.

Window-shopping was a favorite pastime of hers, and she did so now, looking at all the store windows and the pretty goods within. Luna found a bookshop and looked at all the new titles she had yet to find time to read, lingering there for a long time. She often wished for material goods but knew they were, more often than not, more appealing before they were purchased.

Luna knew that, for most people, the things they owned often ended up owning *them*. It was a vicious cycle of consumerism that certainly kept the economy afloat, but Luna also believed the pursuit of possessions was a source of pain for many, many people.

Besides, she would be dead soon—there was no reason to buy meaningless crap now, if ever there had been, which she doubted.

Walking back to her car, Luna considered the evening's transportation. It was two miles to Pulse's hotel. And though there was plenty of time before she had to be there, she knew she couldn't walk the distance. Not tonight anyway. Luna couldn't exactly go walking around downtown New York with a fire axe in her hand, even if the handle *was* broken in half. She'd have to drive.

For one, mischievous moment she actually considered walking with the axe. What was the worst that could happen, after all? She could be arrested...but that wasn't so bad. At least she knew she wouldn't freeze to death in prison. Alas, she had better, more important things to do tonight than get arrested. Still, the thought tickled her into a chuckle.

Driving would be a pain in the ass. In fact, driving anywhere in New York was like pulling one's eyelashes out one at a time, then dousing the eyes in vinegar and setting fire to them with a match. And the parking was atrocious! She had no clue where she'd be able to leave her car once she made it to the hotel, and beyond that, there was still the problem of carrying the axe out in the open once she'd arrived. Thinking of a quick fix, Luna found a long, rumpled deacon's coat in the back of her car that she could hide the axe under if no one looked at her too closely. And hey—this was New York. It wasn't likely that many people *would* take a close look at her—or anyone else.

Luna put the coat and axe on the front passenger seat and got in her car once more. She laid her bouquet of daisies on the dashboard so they could peek at her as she drove. The sight of them brought a smile to her heart. The car itself was an older model, an off-white station wagon with fake wood siding. But it ran fine, and that was all that mattered to her.

Still looking to kill some time, she rummaged around in a pile of clothes and books in the backseat and found a book to read—a romance novel. An *erotic* romance novel. Just the type of story she liked to immerse herself in to help keep her mind off the harsh realities of life.

She settled back to read by the bright lights of the parking lot.

Time passed as she lost herself in the romantic story. Too much time. Luna started when she realized what time it was. She needed to meet Pulse in a half-hour and it would take that long, maybe longer, to drive to the hotel and find a parking space. Luna tossed the book in the backseat and cranked her car. She pulled out of the parking lot she had called home for the past two weeks and headed for the Times Square Hilton.

Traffic was, of course, a nightmare. She didn't need to be psychic to have known that it would be. The smell of exhaust fumes burned her lungs and the sounds of dozens of honking horns aggravated her, setting her teeth on edge. It took a little longer than a half-hour to reach the hotel, and Luna hoped Pulse had waited for her before trying to go and prevent the crime from happening all by his lonesome. And Luna was smart enough to know that he'd do it, too, if she didn't show up soon.

It was difficult, but she found a parking space only three blocks away from the hotel. She took her coat out and put it on, then, looking around to make sure no one was watching, Luna grabbed the fire axe and put it under her arm beneath the camouflage of the coat. She knew, if anyone was watching her, how suspicious her actions appeared, but there was nothing to be done about it.

She nearly ran the distance to the hotel, and would have if she didn't have the axe to worry about. Luna supposed she could have just left it behind and saved herself the trouble, but she couldn't shake the feeling that she might need it tonight, so she was compelled to bring it along.

When she saw Pulse's dark head towering above the crowd outside the Hilton, she breathed a sigh of relief. He had waited for her after all. And even though the night promised to be dangerous, she still felt an overwhelming eagerness to be with Pulse again. She didn't understand it. She didn't even try to. It was simply a fact and she accepted it, as was her nature.

Luna stopped beside him and tugged on his sleeve. He looked down as if surprised to see her. "Sorry I'm late," she said. "I had to drive."

"Doesn't driving save time?" he asked in a puzzled tone.

"Not in New York it doesn't," she chuckled, before quickly sobering. She caught a big breath that stank of exhaust fumes from the traffic passing by the hotel and sighed. "Are you ready?" she asked, steeling herself for the danger ahead.

"Yes," he answered simply.

"I think I want to get to that alley before John does. You know, just wait on him there. We can hide behind the dumpster — yes, I'm certain there's a dumpster." She thought hard and images bombarded her like flashes from a movie projector. "When John brings his victim into the alley we can stop him and make sure the woman gets to safety."

"Yes. The woman's safety is the most important thing. Violence against women — no matter their profession — is despicable in the extreme. We *will* stop him from harming her." The tone in Pulse's voice assured her that he would accept no other outcome and Luna actually felt genuine trust in his confidence. It was an unusual yet pleasant feeling for her.

"Yes, well, that might be the easy part if you can believe it," Luna admitted reluctantly. "We're going to have one very mad psycho-boy on our hands once we stop him from accomplishing his task. We could be hurt or, worse, killed. Well, *you* could anyway. I'm not going to die tonight."

He glanced at her, a hard look in the wake of her certainty that she would be safe while he might not be. "Leave the murderer to me. Stay out of the way and I will

41

take care of him myself." Pulse then looked beyond her, as if he could already see what was to come and was more than prepared for it.

Luna shivered at the iron resolve she heard in the tone of his voice. In that moment he looked and sounded very dangerous. But she wasn't afraid of him at all—in fact she rather liked knowing that he was powerful and confident. Besides, she was too interested in him to feel any fear, too interested in the pleasurable sensations that raced through her with his nearness. And she had no fear that he would hurt her, no matter how dangerous he might be. He'd already said violence against women was a heinous act, and she believed that *he believed* his own words. That was good enough for her to feel quite at ease.

"We've got less than an hour. We need to get going if we want to do this," she reminded him softly.

Luna was a little surprised when he caught her hand and held it in his. There was again that strange current of electricity that instantly made the hairs on her arms stand on end, an arc of energy that ran from his flesh to hers. She found she liked the feeling, alien though it was, and noticed other strange things...like the pebbles on the ground, which were clinging to the bottoms of her shoes as if shot through with static electricity. And the thick, stinging scent of ozone heavy in the air. It was pretty neat.

Pulse turned them easily, never releasing his hold on her, and began walking in the direction of Chinatown.

"Tell me about yourself," she suggested eagerly, stretching her short legs to keep up with his long strides.

"What do you want to know?" he asked absently.

"Everything," she said with a laugh, seeing how intent he was on the path before them. It was so unusual—and exciting—to be in the presence of one who seemed so in control of himself and his surroundings.

Pulse smiled. She caught it with the corner of her eye and then it was gone. Luna thought he had to be the most handsome man in the world. He could break a girl's heart with such a smile if he wanted to.

"There is not much to tell. I live the simple life of a soldier."

Luna blinked. A soldier? Him? No. He was more than that and she knew it. "Yeah, but you're not just any soldier," she pointed out slyly. "You can't make me believe you're not some officer or something, not just a lowly soldier."

He looked at her as if caught off guard by her words and Luna almost grinned. Almost. She knew better.

"I am an Elder on our Council, it's true. I help guide my people through the war and our way of life," he explained, his voice deep and smooth, like velvet dipped in hot, liquid wax. "I have a duty to my men and I see them through battles as best I can, giving them guidance and motivation as they need it. Other than that, I do live simply enough."

"Beneath the Earth's crust." She remembered his words from the night before.

"Yes," he answered.

Luna shook her head, perplexed. "How come I've never seen another like you? All this time I thought we—humans, I mean—were the only intelligent species on the planet, and then you come along and blow my preconceived notions right out the window."

Pulse held her hand tight in his, never breaking contact, and she realized she liked touching him like this. It felt as though she held a live wire in her hands though.

Power hummed through his skin like a bolt of electricity, shocking her, making her feel strangely high. But the sensation was pleasant, not at all uncomfortable. In fact, it made her feel, well…safe.

"We keep to ourselves and our duty. We do not, as a rule, mingle among humans very often."

"But you're here to…what did you say? Discover for yourself why you fight to protect us humans?" she prodded.

"Yes."

"We can be pretty rotten to each other," she admitted with a bitter twist of her lips. "But we're not all bad. Sometimes it might seem like it, but we're not. There's a lot of beauty in the world if you only look for it."

Pulse eyed her. "I'm surprised that someone with your abilities could feel that way." He was silent for a weighted moment. "Do you ever foresee anything positive or is it always tragic?" he asked gently.

Luna sighed heavily, lowering her eyes to her feet, watching with distracted fascination as the dust on the ground seemed to tremble from the static in the air. "It's always bad," she revealed finally. "Sometimes though, usually when I hit a new city, I have a couple weeks of peace, when the premonitions stop for a while. That's when I can see the beauty and value of our lives. During those times I'm grateful just to be alive and well in the world. Then everything starts up again and I try to make a difference and I always fail. It sucks big-time."

"Have you been this way your whole life?" he asked softly, his voice playing over her like warm silk, soothing but sensual at the same time.

"Just since puberty." She shivered, even though the night was unseasonably warm and she wore her coat. "All the women in my family have had this gift." She laughed derisively. "If you could even call it that. I think it's a curse, myself."

"You speak of your family in the past tense," he observed sagely.

"My grandmother, I never knew. But my mom died six years ago. She waited until I turned eighteen and then killed herself. She couldn't take the visions any more," Luna admitted flatly, emotionlessly, though she still felt the pain of the loss deep in her heart.

Pulse stopped walking and regarded her with all too knowing eyes. She fidgeted nervously under his gaze despite herself. How she hated to look weak, uncomfortable.

"You speak as if this tragedy was an acceptable thing."

Luna shook her head thoughtfully, chewing on her lip. "My mom suffered a lot. She made sure she raised me to take care of myself—she was a good mother despite her despair. It wasn't until I reached adulthood that she finally did what she'd wanted to do ever since I can remember. I'm grateful to her for that, for waiting. But I'm not at all okay with the fact that she took her own life. I understand why she did, but I still don't think it's okay," she explained slowly. "Do you understand?"

"I understand that you are alone." His voice was soft, like a caress. It made her tingle from the top of her head to the tips of her toes.

"I'm not alone." She met his gaze easily now, pushing her pain down into the depths of her. "Oh, okay, so I am," she allowed with a short, wry chuckle. "But I like it that way just fine. It's not a bad thing."

"You shouldn't be alone. You should be sheltered, protected."

Luna groaned then laughed despite herself. "Don't tell me you're gonna be like *that*. Look, the alpha male thing is all well and good in romance novels, but in real life it just doesn't wash." She chuckled again, but despite her mirth was still hyperaware of the tight grasp of his hand on hers, the feel of his hot skin, the strength of his fingers.

"I am only telling you how I feel." He tightened his hand and that electric hum raced from her hand to her heart, making it beat wildly in her breast.

"Well, you don't need to worry about me. I've always been able to take care of myself," she assured him. "Besides, we are *supposed* to be talking about you, not me."

"What else do you want to know?" Pulse asked again.

"Well, like, how are you different from us humans? Besides the height, that is—not very many humans are as frickin' tall as you are."

Pulse seemed to think for a minute before finding the words. "We're faster than you, for one thing. Stronger. More intelligent." Luna snorted but he continued without acknowledging her response. "We are impervious to illness and we heal quickly. We have other abilities—too many to name. Each of us is different, unique in his or her own way, not unlike humans in that respect."

"But you look like us. Are you like us…physically?" She blushed to the roots of her hair.

Pulse's gaze met hers and she definitely saw a wicked spark light behind the brown contacts he wore. It made strange fluttering sensations awaken low in her belly.

"We are physically similar. In *all* the right ways," he emphasized softly.

Luna felt her blush burning her cheeks and she looked away, bowing her head to hide her face from him. "That's cool," she said, not knowing what else to say.

"You have no idea," Pulse said.

Luna heard the desire in his voice. It brushed over her like a living thing, swamping her senses. Making her feel strange and wonderful things. She blushed hotter and kept right on walking, not wanting to break the charged moment between them lest she lose the thrill forever.

Chapter Three

හ

Though he was walking beside her it felt as if he were leading the way. But as they finally made it to Chinatown and approached the alley where the crime was due to take place, Luna halted, bringing him to a stop because he wouldn't release her hand. "It's here," she said, pointing down the dark, dank alley. She was glad to see that her fingers weren't trembling.

It was a long, shadowed and utterly creepy alley. The walls that created it were brick, belonging to the two buildings that stood so close together as to barely leave room for a vagrant to stretch out between them. There was a short dumpster piled high with garbage, filling the alley with the sick odor of decay. The alley dead-ended at a small wooden door, set in the short leg branching off the side of the larger building's L-shaped design. At the end of the L, there was a fence blocking passage to the alley that snaked behind the smaller building. There was no way in or out save the front entrance and that small wooden door.

Luna led Pulse behind the dumpster and squatted down. She had to tug his hand a couple of times to get him to join her there, and when he did he looked so ridiculous that she couldn't hold back a laugh. He was just too tall to crouch like this without looking absurd and his legs were so long that, bent as they were, he looked something like a praying mantis.

"What are you laughing at?" he asked with a growl that was more bark than bite.

"Nothing," she lied and looked away from him with supreme effort.

While she controlled her mirth, Pulse watched her with deepening interest. Luna seemed so small to him...and she *was* small. She couldn't have stood over five feet and she was so thin as to look a little malnourished. She seemed more than fragile, and yet she was strong. So strong. Here she was, a human, waiting to stop a horrible crime from being committed against a total stranger with no thought to her own safety. It was a conundrum he had not encountered in the race of humans. A puzzle and a surprise. Just as she was. He wanted to discover her secrets, understand everything about her.

She fascinated him. On every conceivable level.

Of course her appeal didn't center solely on her looks, but they were quite stirring nonetheless. Her hair was riveting. It was the most beautiful shade of blonde he'd ever seen—almost white it was so pale. It was in a thick braid down her back and Pulse instinctively knew that she'd fixed her hair that way on purpose, to give their enemy less of a chance to hurt her by pulling at her loose locks. She was so casually intelligent it surprised him. He'd never really thought of humans as entirely intelligent beings.

The color of her eyes entranced him as well—he'd never seen eyes that color before. They were a light blue with rims of darker blue outlining the iris and pupil. Her lashes were thick and blonde, brightening her gaze further. Her eyes looked like those of an enchantress to him, full of secrets and magic. So strange and exotic, especially to a warrior like himself who was so used to seeing the Shikar eyes of his own race.

And those mystical eyes held such hope within their endless depths. There was such a strong sense of hope about her entire self that it hurt his heart to know that he had, even for a moment, felt condescension for her humanity upon meeting her. Even though she should have been jaded beyond belief given the tragedies of her life, she still tried to make the world a little better for those around her with a selflessness that surprised him. It was clear that she wanted to make a difference, any difference, so long as it was positive. She was a surprise to him in every way.

He hadn't expected to ever meet anyone like her. Luna was a human with superhuman gifts, and a will that was as strong as any he'd ever seen in his own warriors. She didn't care about the dangers to herself, only to others—and it showed in everything she did.

He had to know more, understand as much as he could about her. "You said you know how you die. Do you know when?" he asked, keeping his voice soft in the dark, needing to know her answer yet fearing it at the same time.

Luna looked at him, surprised that he had asked the question. "I don't know. But I'm sure it will be soon," she admitted without fear, shrugging her shoulders in the nonchalant way he was quickly becoming familiar with.

"How can you live like that?" He felt a deep pain for the suffering he knew she must endure with such knowledge. "Knowing what you know?"

Luna glanced down the alley from around the edge of the dumpster then turned back to look at him with her exotic eyes, and he found to his dismay that he almost couldn't meet her gaze.

"It won't be long now," she murmured. She put a finger to his lips and a sudden spark lit the darkness. She jerked her hand back at the sting, but gave him a hard glare to keep him from repeating his question. "I don't worry about my future. Everyone dies eventually. I just happen to know *how* I'll die. There's almost a comfort in that, really. It makes me feel invincible, knowing that I won't die yet, no matter what I do."

"It makes you too impulsive," he said, remembering how she had brazenly walked out into traffic the night before, without a whit of care for her own safety. She was braver than any warrior he'd ever known...or perhaps she was simply foolish. He couldn't decide and he didn't know which he would have preferred be the truth.

"Nah. I've always been impulsive. Now I'm just...unconcerned, I guess you could say. At least about my own safety."

Pulse wanted to ask her more questions but Luna shushed him again. He realized that no one had ever shushed him. In fact, no one had ever dared command him to do anything. And yet...he found that he did not care, so long as the commands came from her lips.

"He's coming," she whispered softly, turning to peek around the dumpster once again.

The sound of low, seductive laughter interrupted their weighty silence. Two forms entered the alley, a man and a woman, both hidden from view by the deep shadows. They embraced, the woman leaning back against the dingy wall while the man's hand wandered up her miniskirt. The woman moaned, the sound plastic and unemotional, and she pulled the man's head down to her breast, which she had bared to the night wind. The man's hand roughly squeezed the exposed globe, his fingers twisting her nipple until she moaned again, this time with sincere desire.

The woman thrust her fingers into the man's shaggy hair and pulled his head back up. She slanted her rouged lips over his, thrusting her tongue deep into his mouth, and the sounds of their intimacy made Luna tremble in mounting fear. Fear for the woman. Fear for what she knew could not end well.

Luna knew that if they didn't do something soon the man would pull out a large hunting knife—he'd killed his own father with that same knife, she felt certain—and slit the woman from throat to belly. Then he would finish having sex with the lifeless body before leaving it limp and forgotten on the dirty ground. But Luna didn't know *what* to do to prevent it. No ideas were coming to her. So she winged it, as she did so many other things in life.

Hey, whatever worked, right?

Before Pulse could stop her she jumped up from behind the dumpster. "Oy! Hey you," she said loudly in her best Cockney imitation—she absolutely loved the vernacular of the Brits. "What's all this then?"

Luna saw the shadows move about the man's face and for a moment she saw him as clear as day. He didn't look like a murderer. He looked like the proverbial guy next door. He had brown hair and brown eyes. He was clean-shaven and well dressed—it was apparent he had enough money for designer clothing. Or maybe he stole it. Luna didn't know and didn't really care.

"You should leave," she told the prostitute, who now eyed her with unmistakable irritation.

"I'm not going anywhere." The woman put her arms around her escort. "Find your own man, honey."

The man pulled the knife from out of nowhere. Its blade glinted in the moonlight, very large and very deadly. The woman screamed as he raised it high, fully intending to do his business despite Luna's presence.

Furious, Luna rushed him. He turned, his prey forgotten, and shoved her back with brutal force, a fist to her chest. Luna stumbled backward and fell on her rear with a grunt, dropping the nearly forgotten axe to the ground at her side. The prostitute screamed and ran for her life while her would-be murderer was otherwise occupied.

The man growled, a sick, menacing sound. He stood over Luna and once more raised his knife high over his head. She watched him calmly, secure in the knowledge that he wouldn't be able to kill her. And she was right. Pulse appeared in the shadows between her and the killer, his presence intimidating and dangerous—far more dangerous than the killer's.

With seemingly little effort, Pulse knocked the knife out of the man's hand and a violent arc of silver lightning lit the alley—its source, the blow of Pulse's hand to the murderer's wrist. Luna felt sure she heard some bones break as blinding spots from the lightning danced dizzyingly in her field of vision. The man screamed, then choked when Pulse grabbed him with a hand to his throat. He lifted the man into the air and easily threw him against a wall, which he bounced off of, flying several feet before landing hard in a dirty puddle of scum on the pavement.

Pulse bent over the crumpled killer. Then the hairs on Luna's body stood on end, as if her entire body was charged with static electricity. The air hummed and smelled heavily of ozone, tickling her nose, making her eyes water. She watched in fascination as Pulse let his hand hover over the murderer's head. A bright arc of electricity danced from his fingertips and into the man's skull. The man screamed and jerked violently, his hair beginning to smoke before his body stilled and, at last, lay limp on the ground.

Pulse turned and immediately helped her to her feet. Luna let him, never taking her eyes off the fallen murderer, jumping nervously as the body jerked convulsively in the muck. "Did you kill him?" she asked shrilly. Even though the man was truly evil, she didn't want to think that she'd helped bring about his execution.

"No," Pulse said, glancing back at the body on the ground at his feet. "I just burned his mind."

He sounded so casual that her mind boggled. "How did you do that?" She swallowed hard, dazed. "I saw...*something* come out of your fingertips!"

Pulse ran his hands over her and she choked on her words. When he touched her, a mild electric shock raced through her body and it continued to hum deliciously as he roved his hands all over her body, checking for injuries.

"I'm fine," she said, trying and failing to brush his wandering hands away. "I'm not hurt, chill out." Her heart was racing fast and desire grew like a weight in her tummy. When he touched her she lost all rational thought, pulling her away from the horrible reality of the man lying mere feet away, smoking as if he were burning from the inside. In a daze, she welcomed the comfort of Pulse's touch, yet in the back of her mind she wondered how he could touch her so gently when such deadly magic flowed forth from those same hands with nothing but the force of his will. She wondered what it would be like if he touched her in passion, and shivered.

"You're cold," he said, and his voice soothed her further.

"No," she laughed, then immediately sobered. "I'm actually hot. This coat is too heavy for this kind of weather."

"But you shivered," he countered, watching her carefully.

"Delayed reaction, I guess," she lied easily. But she could tell by the arrogant, totally satisfied male look in his eyes that he knew her lie for what it was.

He was far, far too sensual. And what was more, Luna knew he was aware of that truth just as much as she was.

What a strange, strange night this was turning out to be.

Luna knew, too, it was about to get even stranger.

"Freeze!"

Luna gasped and immediately bent to retrieve her weapon, knowing that the officer who'd spotted them would not be able to clearly see what she was doing. She hefted the axe in her hand and ran swiftly to the door at the end of the alley, secure in the knowledge that the policeman—new to the force—would not fire on them. Wasting no time, she chopped through the wood with a speed and strength that surprised her and put her arm into the gaping hole, unlocking the door so they could escape through it.

Pulse watched her as if he were studying a lab animal. He seemed amused by her antics, utterly detached from the threat of the cop who even now pursued them, and she felt her temper flare. "Come on," she called, aggravated at his stillness, going through the door with only a backward glance. Pulse sighed heavily and followed her, ignoring the shrill yells of the police officer behind him.

Even though Luna had begun running the instant she entered the dirty, crowded warehouse, Pulse caught up to her easily. He grabbed her hand and spun her around dizzily to face him. "Where are you going?" he asked with seemingly mild curiosity.

"I'm trying to find a way out of this place, you r-tard!" she said shrilly as a bright light zeroed in on them. The cop had followed, spotting them with his flashlight. She tugged, panicked, trying to get Pulse to follow her, but he would not let go of her hand and he would not be moved.

Pulse pulled her against him. She heard the beat of his heart against her ear and the sound was oddly soothing, especially considering the circumstances, damn him. But in a blink of an eye, those surroundings disappeared like a puff of smoke in the wind and she cried out, clutching him tight as the floor dropped out from under her feet.

There was a moment when she felt as though she were flying through space. It was a disquieting sensation, setting her teeth on edge, but Pulse held her tight and safe against him and she trusted that the feeling would pass.

She blinked and found herself in Pulse's hotel room. "Groovy," she murmured, unable to think of any other intelligent word, praying to every god she knew of that she wouldn't faint.

"Are you hurt?" he asked with some concern.

"No. I'm fine, don't worry about me. It's all good." She put her hand to her head and swayed dizzily, thankful that he still held her or she knew she would have fallen. "Man, but that was wild, wasn't it? We managed to stop the killer *and* get away from the cops! Can you do that at will? I mean, disappear from one place and reappear in another?" Sheesh, how she hated her habit of rambling when her adrenaline was high. But she tamped down on the buzz of her post-battle excitement with effort and distractedly tapped the end of the fire axe against the plush carpet.

"Yes," he answered, releasing her with a slowness that made her more than aware of the touch of his fingers through her clothing. "But I try not to do so too often. Traveling tires even the strongest."

Luna walked deeper into the room and sat on the edge of Pulse's bed, watching absently as he sat in a chair beside her. "Traveling? Is that what you call it?" she asked weakly, feeling both tired and energized after the events of the past hour.

"Yes. It is like folding space and time together at once. It allows us to go anywhere at any time, so long as we have a clear destination in mind."

"It's a good name for it." She swallowed, mouth gone dry. "Can all Shikars do that?"

Pulse shook his dark head. "No. Not all."

"Well, you learn something new every day," she quipped cockily with a bravado she didn't exactly feel. Then she fell silent, not knowing what else to say. At last, feeling uncomfortable beneath his penetrating gaze, she rose to her feet again. "Well, I guess I better get on out of here."

"I will walk you to your car," he said, rising with her, towering over her, making her feel a little overwhelmed by his fascinating presence and his very masculine appeal.

"You don't have to do that," she said hurriedly, nervous suddenly for reasons she couldn't explain.

"I want to," he answered firmly.

Luna smiled, giving in, knowing she didn't want to say goodbye yet anyway. "Okay." She shrugged and turned to the door.

Pulse beat her to it, opening the door for her gallantly. When she passed through it, he grabbed her hand and held it in his once more. There was that electric hum again and Luna's nipples grew hard, her breasts heavy. She hunched her shoulders forward to hide the telltale signs of her arousal, but knew that it wouldn't fool him for a minute.

They walked to the elevator together, hands clasped as if they would never part again, and for the first time in a long time, Luna didn't feel so alone.

Chapter Four

ଚ

"What will you do now?" he asked her once they were outside again.

Luna matched her strides to his, holding her axe under her arm to keep it hidden. "There's going to be a fire in a restaurant not too far from here around noon tomorrow. I was going to go and pull the fire alarm a few minutes before the flames started. I'm hoping that maybe people will leave the building before it's too late, you know?"

"I do not like knowing you will do this alone," he said haltingly, as if the words pained him.

"There's no danger. Not for me anyway," she rushed to assure him.

"Still, it sits uneasy with me."

"Don't worry. I'll be fine. And hopefully the ten people who are due to die tomorrow will be, too," she said with an easy confidence she did not feel.

"Will you come to see me tomorrow night?" he asked, and Luna clearly heard the desire and hope in his voice and was warmed by it most pleasantly.

She didn't ask where he would be during the day. It wasn't any of her business after all. Yeah, right. As if that had ever stopped her. Yet, she didn't want to press him too hard. She didn't know if he'd take much more of her prodding.

"Well, tomorrow night there's going to be a bank robbery upstate. Two security guards are going to get shot—one of them will eventually die of his wounds, leaving behind a wife and five kids. I was thinking about giving the cops an anonymous tip and dropping by to check if they follow up on the information or not. You could come with me. After all, you're kind of like my good luck talisman now." She smiled at him shyly, swinging their clasped hands back and forth with a gaiety that belied the severity of her prediction.

"How do you do it?" he asked her once again, frowning down at her from his great height.

"Do what?" she asked, not really paying attention to his words so much as the sensual depth of his voice.

"Find happiness even though there is sadness and horror all around you," he explained, as if his question should have been obvious.

Luna shrugged, as was her habit. "Quit asking me that! I don't know. I'm not always like this, you know. I have my doubts and worries. Sometimes I just feel like living is a hopeless nightmare that I'll wake up from someday—if I'm lucky. But…I don't know…when you're with me, I feel happy. Just knowing you is like knowing a great secret. It gives me some hope that not all of life is a lonesome struggle, you know? Not if there are magical people like you living among us." She felt no shame in laying her thoughts bare to this man. She knew in her blood that she could trust him to understand.

"You surprise me," he admitted haltingly. "I did not expect that from a human."

"Yeah, well, I'm full of surprises, trust me," she laughed, feeling silly. "You'll get sick of all the surprises if you hang around me for too long."

They approached her station wagon and she opened the backseat door to throw the axe inside. Pulse looked into the vehicle with a great show of interest, finally releasing her hand. "You have a lot of things in your car," he observed quietly, as if choosing his words with care.

"Yeah, well, that's all my stuff. I'm kind've living out of my car right now," she admitted absently.

She should have been as careful.

Pulse turned to look at her so fast that his hair fanned out behind him. "You live here? In this vehicle? This is *where you live*!?"

He kept repeating himself, as if he just couldn't believe it. Luna realized she should have expected this reaction and nearly kicked herself for telling him. But then she laughed. She couldn't help it. He was adorable in his incredulity. "Yeah. In this vehicle." She repeated his words, mimicking him almost perfectly.

"I cannot allow that," he said arrogantly, his broad shoulders straightening proudly.

She laughed again. "Well, that's too bad, because facts are facts and it's a fact that I live in this car."

"You shouldn't live like this," he pressed stubbornly, eyes fierce.

"Deal with it already," she said shortly, growing uncomfortable. More than she cared to admit. She wasn't ashamed to live in her car. But Pulse was reacting like she'd confided an evil sin, and it made her feel as if she were no more than a bum. And she supposed she was in a way. But she preferred to think of her lifestyle as bohemian, not slumming.

"You will come back with me, to my hotel," he said, grabbing her hand again and tugging, giving her no choice but to follow him.

"Stop it." She struggled to pull free, but he held her with a strength she couldn't overpower. "Stop it right now!"

Pulse turned to her and she tripped to a halt beside him. "How long have you lived like this?"

"I don't want to talk about this anymore," she nearly shouted, feeling cornered, still tugging her hand.

"I do not care," he said ruthlessly, keeping her hand captive in his. "Tell me. How long has it been since you slept in a bed, with a proper roof over your head?"

Luna had to think. "I don't know. A year maybe." She shrugged carelessly. "It doesn't matter," she assured him.

"It matters," he growled. "You are a woman. You should be cared for, have all your needs seen to. You should be protected."

"Oh, give me a break." She rolled her eyes. "Just because I'm a woman doesn't mean I can't rough it now and then."

"Now and then?" he asked incredulously, his face a puzzle of shock and disbelief. "You've been living like this for a year—and by your own admission you're not even sure of *that*. No. This is unacceptable. You're coming with me." He turned and began walking again, dragging her relentlessly behind him.

"Let go of me," she grunted, pulling at her captured hand. "I said let go!" She kicked him on the back of his leg as hard as she could.

Pulse merely grunted and continued on his way.

"Pulse, you're being unreasonable about this," she said, trying a different tactic. "Trust me, I'm safe and comfortable in my car. Really. I sleep the day away in a ride-share parking lot. It's very open so there isn't much danger of me being disturbed by troublemakers, and it's quiet. Calm. Almost peaceful." She knew she was laying it on thick, but she couldn't stand having him tell her what to do or where she was going to stay for the rest of the night.

"I will not allow you to do this, not for one more day," he said firmly.

She jerked him to a stop. He had to stop—if not, he would have had to drag her behind him like a rag doll. "I'm not going anywhere," she said stubbornly, digging her heels in determinedly.

Pulse glared at her. He moved so fast she couldn't stop him. He bent and threw her over his shoulder, bouncing her so that her teeth jarred in her head. "What are you doing? Let me go!" she shrieked, pounding her fists into his back as she dangled over his broad shoulder.

The world fell away again and she choked her cries back with a surprised grunt as the G-force hit her like a thousand-ton weight against her chest. Of course, the sensation passed and they reappeared inside Pulse's hotel room. Luna growled and pounded his back once more for good measure. "You great big jerk," she growled fiercely. "I take back all the nice stuff I said about you."

He tossed her unceremoniously onto the bed. "You will sleep there. I will sleep in the chair," he said, ignoring her sputtered protests.

Luna didn't know whether to scream or cry. She definitely did not like being told what to do, that much was certain. And she'd been so happy not moments ago…it was a loss she felt keenly. "Just so you know, I'm doing this under protest," she said petulantly.

"Your protest is duly noted," he shot back. "But you *will* sleep here, where it's safe and comfortable."

She stuck her tongue out at him rebelliously. "Do you tell all women what to do?" she asked grumpily, settling back against the pillows. The bed really *was* comfortable, she noted with reluctance.

"Yes. And they don't make a fuss like you do," he accused pointedly.

"What do you expect? I hardly know you, but after two nights together you think you know what's best for me? Well, you don't," she insisted, punching a pillow for emphasis. "I don't need a babysitter. Especially not one like you," she sneered angrily.

Pulse glared at her. "What do you mean by that?" He put his hands on his hips in a show of mounting frustration and Luna almost laughed, but she thought better of it just in time. No doubt he'd take great exception to her laughter at the moment.

Luna snorted instead. "You're arrogant and stuck-up. You act all high and mighty, as if you rule the world. Well, you don't. We do—*humans* do. And there's nothing your cute little Shikar butt can do about it."

Pulse looked truly horrified by her words. "Well, you're a little brat," he shot back, remembering the human invective from his last trip to the Territories. "You're ungrateful and stubborn and difficult to get along with."

"No one said you had to save me," she pointed out, feeling a painful crack begin in her heart. "Besides, I'm not difficult to get along with—you are!"

With a growl he sat down heavily in the chair by the bed. "You drive me mad, woman." He put his head in his hands so that his hair fell like a dark curtain over his features.

"Yeah, well, welcome to my world," she shot back, crossing her arms over her chest and crossing her ankles on the mattress sullenly, deliberately looking anywhere but at him. The pain in her heart was so terrible that she had a hurtful lump in her throat she could barely speak around. She didn't understand her reaction.

They were silent for a long time, testing each other's resolve, their wills waging a silent battle for dominance. Finally, too tired to hold on to her anger, Luna sighed heavily and looked at Pulse. "Look, I'm sorry if I seem ungrateful. It's super nice of you to offer your room and bed to someone you only just met last night. It's just that I don't like people telling me what to do."

Pulse nodded his understanding. "And I, too, am sorry for being difficult to get along with."

"You're not that bad," she allowed, knowing how unfair she'd been. "You're just…well, *you*."

Pulse brushed his hair back from his face, and the gesture was so casually sexy her legs clenched tight. "I have never been spoken to so insolently as I have since meeting you."

"Yeah, well, I'm like that," she quipped and barked a laugh despite herself. "Truce?"

"A truce," he agreed. "Now I shall order us something to eat. Look at the menu there and tell me what you want."

"I've already eaten tonight."

"Eat again," he said stonily.

Luna sighed and threw her hands up in a show of surrender. "Okay. Here, lemme see." She picked up the menu from the bedside table, trying and failing to ignore just how expensive the cuisine was. "I'll have the chicken fingers and a salad," she decided at last.

Pulse called room service and placed their order—he requested the lamb. Luna reached into her back pocket for her wallet and pulled out thirty dollars. "Here," she said, handing the money to him.

"I have no need of your money," he said, clearly affronted.

"Take it," she pressed.

"No. It is not necessary, I assure you. In your world I am considered a very wealthy man."

Luna frowned. "How do you get money?"

"We Shikars have been part of the human economy since its inception. Indeed, I am told that we are responsible for it. We have money invested all over the world and vaults full of gold, which I am assured are of great worth. Our people, our civilization, have evolved beyond the use of money, however. We only need it when we come to the surface for any extended period of time, and there's always plenty to go around."

"Well spank my butt and call me Susie. You don't have to worry about money? Dang, that must be nice."

He looked a little confused by her words, as she'd known he would be. "We are all equal in my world. Wealth has no meaning, only duty and honor," he said quietly.

Luna watched him from beneath her lashes. God, but he was handsome. His proximity was doing something funny to her insides, and she felt as if the air was charged with static electricity. She realized with a start that it actually was—Pulse was emitting a low-frequency charge of electricity that hummed all around them. She could feel it as plain as day. She squirmed in her seat, ignoring the heat that stained her face. Being this close to Pulse was like being near a live wire—a very seductive, sensual and appealing live wire that made her heart race and her palms sweat.

She scooted down the bed and reclined with her head propped up on one hand. "Tell me about a day in the life of Pulse," she said.

Pulse's gaze met hers. "I meet with my fellow Council members at the start of each day. We discuss many things— the war, the food supply, the concerns of our people. We come to many decisions and implement them immediately. The rest of the day I have meetings with my men, warriors who either fight alone or in groups. We discuss strategy and purpose and then I send them on their way."

"Do some of them die in this war?" she asked softly, then winced, immediately regretting her words when she realized how insensitive such a question might seem, though she hadn't intended it to be.

"Yes," Pulse murmured, his voice low and without joy. "But we honor our fallen warriors. We provide for their families and remember them always. We're not like humans—we don't forget those who give their lives to protect us."

"Not all humans are like that," she protested immediately.

"Most of them are," he said, seeming to challenge her to deny it.

She couldn't. "Maybe you're right. But we humans have a lot going on. We have very busy lives. It's hard, sometimes, to stop and give a little prayer of thanks for our soldiers. But that doesn't mean we don't honor them in our hearts."

"Our people lead very different lives," he observed. "Where your people are motivated by wealth and status, we are humble, simple folk who aid each other whenever possible or necessary."

Luna eyed him carefully. "You really *have* lost faith in mankind. What will you do if you can't find something that redeems us in your eyes? Will you stop protecting us from the monsters?"

"There are still those of us who feel the human race is worth protecting. If I cannot find evidence to make me believe that that is true, I will resign from the Council and take a post watching the Gates for Daemon threat."

She felt something wrench inside her at the thought that Pulse would change his life so drastically if he couldn't find what he sought. Luna determined then and there that she would make sure he believed in the good of mankind before he left to return to his home.

The thought of Pulse returning home made her feel a little lonely.

A knock sounded at the door. Their dinner had arrived.

Chapter Five

ॐ

It was the best meal she'd eaten in recent memory. She ate everything — the chicken, the fries, the salad and an ice-cold bottle of Coke. For the first time in a long time she felt truly full. She finished her meal long before Pulse finished his, so she settled back on the bed amongst the plush pillows and watched him eat.

"You don't eat nearly enough," he told her, eying her empty plates. "You're wasting away."

Luna laughed and ran her hand over what she thought of as her Buddha belly. "I eat enough. And I won't waste away, I can promise you that."

"I have thought it over and I have decided you may go and try to stop that fire tomorrow. But you are to return here immediately after you do."

She choked on her shock. "You can't tell me what to do," she explained in exasperation. "I'll go to the restaurant tomorrow and I'll come back here, but I'll do those things because I *choose* to. Not because you command me to."

The hairs on the nape of her neck stood on end as his gaze met hers. "You will not try to run?" he asked, and there was a clear warning in his voice that she should answer in the way he wanted her to or else.

"No," she answered truthfully. "I'm too interested in what you're doing to duck out now."

"Good," he said and continued eating.

She watched him with great interest. Every move he made was precise, elegant and overtly sensual. His masculinity was a potent presence in the room, making her breathing speed up and her heart race. She could smell his scent over the smell of their meal, and it made her mouth water as no mere dish of food ever could.

He smelled terrific. Like rain and tree bark and herbs all mixed together. It was a potent aphrodisiac and she caught herself sniffing the air just to capture a trace of his natural perfume within her nostrils.

She lay down and closed her eyes. Luna could no longer watch him without wanting him. She wondered with great interest if Shikars had sex the same way humans did. There was a brief moment when she thought to ask him, but she caught her curiosity in time. She didn't want him to think she was too eager.

But it had been years since she'd been with a man. She couldn't even remember the last time. And her appetite for sex could be enormous at times. She was no saint, nor did she profess to be one. Luna was a hot-blooded woman with needs just like everyone else, needs that sometimes rode her hard and relentlessly. Like now. Just watching Pulse eat was titillating in the extreme. Being this close to him made her fingers itch to touch him.

Luna rolled over on her side, giving Pulse her back. She sighed heavily and snuggled her head into the pillow. Moments later, sleep claimed her, coming over her like a thick, welcomed blanket.

As she fell into dreaming, Pulse watched over her, thoughts racing, until the sun rose behind the room's thick curtains and he finally found his rest as well.

* * * * *

Luna woke up and instantly realized where she was and who she was with. She rolled over in the bed and turned to look at Pulse who sat, head bent to the side against the chair, deeply asleep.

With his eyes closed, Luna saw how long and dark his lashes were and felt a spurt of jealousy. She'd always wanted lashes like that. His face was smooth without the mask of discipline he wore, giving him a younger look. Even with the streaks of silver in his hair he looked no older than thirty. The golden bronze of his skin was less brilliant in the darkness of the enclosed room, but she could easily picture it in her mind.

Luna rose and went to the window. She threw aside the curtains, letting in some sunlight so that she could better study him as he slept. Luna was careful not to let the brightness hit his eyes for fear of waking him, but a streak of warm, golden light fell on his outstretched legs.

Pulse awoke with a snarl, startling Luna violently. He disappeared from the chair and reappeared deeper in the room beyond the reach of the sun. "What are you doing, woman?" he exclaimed harshly.

Luna had no idea what was wrong with him. "I was just letting in some sunlight."

"We Shikars cannot stand the sun. Our skin burns in its rays, most painfully. Are you trying to kill me?"

With a harrumph she closed the drapes, casting the room into darkness once more. "I didn't know. I mean, how could I? You didn't tell me."

Pulse took a deep, audible breath and let it out. "You are right. I should have said something before the sun rose. You had no idea what you were doing. I apologize for chastising you."

Luna nodded her head to let him know she accepted his apology. "I didn't hurt you too badly, did I?" she asked with some concern now that her surprise had faded.

Pulse shook his head, sending his hair fanning out around him. "No. I just got a little hot, that is all."

Grabbing the end of her braid, Luna began to undo her hair. Pulse watched her every move like a hawk regarding its prey. "Good. Uh...I'm going to take a shower if you don't mind," she said, feeling uncomfortable beneath his gaze. "I've got some time to kill before the fire today."

Pulse motioned towards the bathroom. "Please, be my guest."

As she passed close to him on her way to the shower, the hairs on her body stood at attention and the smell of ozone was heavy in the air. She'd noticed that about him — whenever he felt any strong emotion, he let loose some of that electrical power she'd witnessed the night before.

After closing the bathroom door, Luna sighed and leaned heavily against it. It was hard work, being around a guy like Pulse. He was just so...male. His presence alone demanded respect and obedience, it seemed. She couldn't help but wonder what kind of commander he was with his troops. A formidable one, no doubt. *He certainly is with me,* she thought, remembering the events of the night before.

Luna removed her clothes and folded them carefully, laying them on top of the toilet tank. She didn't have a change of clothes so she'd have to put those back on. But she was all right with that — what mattered most to her now was the unlimited shower time she had to look forward to.

She turned on the spray and adjusted the temperature until it was as hot as she liked it. And she liked it very hot. Then she stepped under the spray, letting the steaming water run down her hair and body. She shivered deliciously and her muscles immediately relaxed, bringing forth a heartfelt sigh of pleasure from her lips.

The water sluiced over her, each rivulet running down the planes and curves of her body like the finger of a curious lover. Luna rubbed her soapy hands over her breasts, wincing at the tenderness of her stiff, puffy nipples. Nipples that had been perpetually hard since meeting Pulse, it seemed. The hot spray tickled over her scalp, a massage that heightened all her senses, so that soon she was tingling all over and it had nothing to do with the heat of the water.

Electricity hummed thickly in the air. Pulse was close. She let herself imagine that he was in the shower with her and that the water was his hands, exploring her every secret place. The throbbing ache between her legs, the trembling of her buttocks, the heavy tingle of her breasts and the desperate stab of her nipples. She imagined him suckling her there, biting her there, rubbing his face all over her chest and moving down beyond.

Her orgasm shook her, surprised her, and made her knees weak and liquid like warm honey in summer heat. It was a soft orgasm, but it made her entire body thrum. Starlight burned through her blood and she felt the great chasm of the cosmos that she was so much a part of, felt every being within it and knew what it was like to be one with the universe, if only for a brief second.

Coming down was hard and jarring, but inevitable. So she lingered for an hour in the shower, hanging on to the sweetness of her release as long as she was able. It was the first time in a long time that Luna had been afforded such a sweet taste of paradise.

The freedom of the long shower was a treat she did not take for granted, either. The showers she'd been taking at the truck stop were effective enough, but there was always the feeling of being rushed. Here she could take her time and enjoy what had only become a quick, everyday chore in her normal life.

Outside, Pulse listened to the sound of her bathing through the door. Ear pressed to the wood, he sighed softly as he heard the water hitting her skin. His cock was hard and heavy and he palmed himself through the soft cloth of his trousers. Desire rode him hard, demanding that he take the human woman who was so unsuspectingly taking a shower in the next room. He tamped down on the urge to break open the door and join her in the bath, but with much effort.

He really wanted her. More than he had at first even dared to realize.

There was such fire, such life in her. Luna was unlike anyone he'd ever met—and he was over four hundred years old. She captured his thoughts and his imagination, making him feel more alive when he was with her than he did when he was not.

It was more than just a physical attraction with him, and he recognized it as such. He wanted to possess her, to tame her raw spirit. The thought of being one with so strong a person was extremely titillating. He knew he would never have to hide anything from her—she would understand anything, no matter the situation. Luna was used to adaptation, to change. She was so smart, so clever it surprised him. She could very well be as intelligent as any Shikar, and he knew it despite his years of prejudice to the contrary where humans were concerned.

He left his position at the bathroom door and paced the room with mounting frustration. He wanted her now, but Pulse knew that humans needed more time, more patience when it came to matters of the flesh and heart. There was nothing for it. He would have to wait and go at her pace. It would be difficult, but he was up for the challenge.

He sat in his chair and waited for her to finish bathing.

When Luna finally emerged from the shower her skin was pink all over from the heat. The room was full of steam, the mirror over the sink obscured by it. Luna didn't see anything resembling a comb lying about, so she ran her fingers through her hair to detangle it. She put it up in a ponytail, pulling it tight on her head. It dripped down her back and she used a towel to dry the ends.

She wiped away the steam on the mirror, streaking it. Smiling at her reflection, she dried the rest of her pink body. Her nipples were fully erect and swollen, and when she ran the towel over them another spark of desire ignited within her. Pulse immediately came to mind once more and she chuckled at her own fancy. With the tips of her fingers, she squeezed the long, thick crests of her breasts, making them stand even more erect. She chuckled again and finished drying herself before once more putting her clothes back on.

When she stepped out of the bathroom, the air felt cool on her flushed skin and she breathed it deeply into her lungs. Pulse had risen from his seat the moment she entered the room, and he had a strange look in his eyes that puzzled her.

"What?" she asked, automatically putting her hand to her hair, smoothing the tail with long, calming strokes.

He rushed her. Luna had time to make one squeak of surprise before she was in his arms and his mouth slammed down on hers. It was as though a bolt of lightning filled her, shocking her from head to toe, bringing all of her senses screaming to life.

Overwhelmed by her own passionate response, she threw her arms around his neck and began to kiss him back. His tongue entered her mouth, playing with her own, swamping her with his exotic flavor. He pressed the length of his body to hers, lifting her against the wall so that he didn't have to lean down so much to claim possession of her lips.

Luna gasped, feeling his thick, hard cock pressing tight against her belly. Their breath mingled until she didn't know where hers ended and his began. Her body began to quiver, hot, heavy and needy, and she held tighter to him so as not to get lost in the storm of passion he awoke within her.

One of his hands moved to cup her breast. She knew he could feel the stab of her nipple, even through the layers of clothes she wore. She gasped when he zeroed in on it, pinching and tugging it delicately—just as she'd imagined he would—until she was breathless. His lips slanted over hers, deepening their kiss, and his clever fingers stroked her breast from base to tip, over and over again. She moaned brokenly into his mouth and he swallowed the sound hungrily.

When he pulled away she almost followed him, wanting the kiss to never end. Luna opened her eyes and met his gaze with hers and the desire she saw in the depths of that gaze shook her to her core.

"Take out your contacts," she demanded breathlessly. "I want to see your eyes."

Pulse hesitated, as if he didn't want to let her go. Then he turned, giving her his back as he carefully took out the colored lenses. He went to the table at the bedside and put them in their proper case so as not to damage them. He realized his hands were shaking with need and almost laughed at his boyish lack of control. Taking a deep breath, Pulse once more turned to her and regarded her with naked eyes.

Luna gasped. His eyes were deep, golden amber with streaks of red and orange fire throughout. Framed by his long, dark lashes, the eyes were striking—almost glowing they were so clear and bright. He had similar eyes as the monsters of her youth, she realized with some surprise. Though his were much, much more beautiful.

She went to him and flung her arms about his neck, pulling his head down for another kiss. But they kept their eyes open this time, staring deep into each other's souls. Luna gently nibbled his full lower lip and he growled, grabbing her tight against him. His tongue invaded her mouth to pillage and conquer, laying waste to all her senses at once.

Her body was trembling and with each stroke of his tongue against hers she felt an electric jolt of passion burn through her, making her knees go weak. He held her up with his easy strength, keeping her from collapsing bonelessly against him. One of his arms gathered her close and with his free hand he cupped her face gently, positioning her just so and deepening the kiss until they were both breathless.

They broke apart too quickly, both knowing that if they let the kiss go any further they would lose their control. Luna, panting, eyed the bed and wondered if losing control wouldn't be such a bad thing. She was tempted— oh, how she was tempted!—but she finally caught her breath again and knew that the moment wasn't right.

She had a mission, after all. And it was almost time for her to be ready for that mission. There was simply no time for sex, though she wanted it so much her teeth ached. Sex would have to come later. And she vowed fervently to herself that it *would* happen. Luna would make certain that it did.

"I have to go," she said softly and skirted around him to retrieve her shoes.

"You'll come back?" he asked in a gravelly voice.

"I will," she said, meeting his superheated gaze. "I promise."

"Be careful."

Luna nodded. "I will. Don't worry. Nothing will happen to me."

"I will wait for your return," he said with a small nod of his head.

The room was charged with static electricity—she shocked herself when she grabbed her keys from the bedside table, where she'd placed them the night before. All the dry hairs on her body were standing on end and her skin tingled as if it had been touched with a live wire.

Luna liked knowing that his control slipped in her arms. Oh yes, she did like that. She sat on the edge of the bed and put her socks and tennis shoes on without looking at him—he was just too much of a temptation. With a sigh, she rose to her feet. "I'm going," she said. Pulse was between her and the door.

Pulse stepped aside, but when she passed him her arm brushed his, sending a shock resounding through her. She opened the door and looked at the number on the front, so she could find her way back, and stepped through it, shutting it softly behind her.

Pulse watched her go, felt her go, and had to keep himself from stopping her. He would not be able to go to her aid if she needed him, with the sun still so high in the sky. He'd sent so many off to battle that it was with stunned surprise he realized he was worried about her, and would be until she returned. She was no warrior—she was his woman. And to think that he had let her go…the long day without her would be torture for him.

He went back to his chair and sat down, waiting. He would count the minutes until she came back to him.

Chapter Six

ഇ

The restaurant was small and cozy—she hadn't expected that. It was full of people enjoying their food and each other's company. Though this was the type of place she could never afford to frequent, she noted that the customers were just regular men and women, people not unlike herself, clearly not all of them rich moguls as she had subconsciously expected.

In order to gain entry, she posed as a normal customer and waited as the hostess found her a seat. She knew the seat would be close to a fire alarm, the same way she knew which customers were slated to die. It was difficult, but Luna did not make eye contact with any of the would-be victims of the fire on her way to her table. It would have been too painful to share a look, a moment, with any of them.

Only Luna knew of the events unfolding in the kitchen. A grease fire would start, only minutes from now, and it would spread throughout the kitchen with a speed that would shock everyone. Except herself. The entire restaurant would be engulfed in flames in a matter of moments, trapping ten unfortunate souls within as it blazed unchecked.

She waited until she was greeted by a waitress and ordered a soda. The waitress went to get her drink and Luna breathed deep, gathering her courage. She made sure no one around her was looking then rose from her seat, quickly grabbed the lever of the fire alarm and pulled. Hard.

The shrieking wail of the alarm caught everyone's attention. Still, no one rose from their seats. The population of the restaurant simply sat where they were, looking around themselves curiously, like calves brought to the slaughter. Even the servers did nothing. They simply continued about their duties despite the noise, fully believing that the fire alarm had accidentally been tripped by some malfunction or human error.

Luna had had enough. There was no time to waste. She stood on her chair, waving her hands about her head madly, hoping to draw people's stares. "Fire," she screamed shrilly, so loud that the word echoed in her own ears like a death knell. "Fire!"

One waitress glared at her as if she though Luna was crazy and Luna supposed she wasn't far off.

"There's nothing to worry about," the waitress said loudly enough for everyone to hear over the noise and slowly mounting confusion. "There's no fire, don't worry, the alarm just tripped, that's all. We'll have it under control in a few minutes, please bear with us."

"No," Luna shouted desperately, jumping from her seat onto the table so that it shuddered beneath her in protest. "*No*. There's a fire in the kitchen and we all have to get out now before this whole place burns down!" Her voice had risen to a broken wail despite her will to control her mounting frenzy.

"Ma'am, I'm going to have to ask you to leave." Luna's waitress had returned and was eyeing her furiously. She reached out her hand to grab Luna's, but Luna backed away before the woman could reach her, teetering dangerously on the table.

"I'm not leaving. There *is* a fire. We have to evacuate the restaurant right away!" Luna looked at her watch and gasped. Two more minutes until the flames started. "*Please.*

We have to hurry," she begged emotionally as her panic mounted.

"I'm going to call the police if you don't get down *now*," her waitress said angrily. The woman's eyes darted to the fire alarm, so close to Luna. "You pulled the alarm, didn't you?" the woman asked with obvious dawning realization.

"We have to get everybody out," Luna cried hoarsely as tears of frustration threatened painfully. "People are going to die!"

One of the male waiters approached. "Get down, ma'am. Now!" he shouted at Luna fiercely.

Luna shook her head and stomped on the table. "Damn it, listen to me!" she roared. "There's a fire!"

The waitress crossed her arms over her chest. "No one's buying it, lady," she yelled balefully. "Now get down or I will call the fucking cops."

Luna looked around the room, seeing all the stares directed at her. No one was listening. They were just watching her display, and the servers who were trying to coax her off the table, with curiosity. The wail of the siren was so loud it grated on Luna's nerves and she knew it had to be just as annoying to everyone else. Still, no one left. No one paid attention. They were all so secure in their little, familiar world they didn't considered that danger could possibly be looming.

The fire had started by now. Luna jumped off the table, past the servers, and ran to a chair by a tall window. Finally people began to rise, questioning looks on their faces that gave Luna some hope. She lifted the chair and shoved it into the glass with wild abandon. Gasps murmured throughout the restaurant as people watched the spectacle with incredulity, but Luna ignored them. She shoved the chair at the glass once more. The tall panel burst into a web of cracks but didn't break. Luna was determined, however, to give the patrons at least one more exit. She lifted the chair again, even as the waiter tried to grab it away from her. With as much strength as she could muster, she heaved the waiter off her and hurled the chair at the window once again. She was rewarded with the sound of glass hitting the floor as the window exploded into a million pieces and the chair flew outside, through the exit she had made.

"You're gonna pay for that!" the waiter shouted over the din. "I'm calling the cops right now, you psycho!"

The smell of smoke tickled her nose. "Everybody get out! *Now!*" Luna was screaming. Desperate for someone to believe her.

The patrons could now smell the smoke as well and seemingly as one, they rose from their seats—only to stand there, looking around as if waiting for further instructions on how to proceed.

Luna growled, her frustration riding her like a freight train. "The exits are that way," she yelled, pointing both in the direction of the main entrance and the one she had made herself.

Smoke billowed out of the kitchen and a cook ran from the room. He looked around wildly and yelled, "Fire! Fire in the kitchen!"

On the heels of his words, a large booming sound rocked the foundation of the restaurant. The door leading to the kitchen blew outward, shooting across the room, hitting the cook and knocking him down brutally. Flames and black smoke blasted out of the open doorway, almost instantly filling the room with noxious fumes.

Screams were overcoming the sound of the still wailing fire alarm as people crammed the doorway of the main exit, trampling each other in a bid to escape the fastest. A second, more violent explosion reverberated in the kitchen and great plumes of black smoke made it impossible to see more than a few feet ahead.

It was happening so fast. Even Luna, who had foreseen it all, was surprised at how swiftly the restaurant filled with smoke, heat and flames, and the press of panicked victims.

Luna had the horrible foresight to know that the CO_2 tanks in the kitchen that supplied the soft drinks with bubbles would also explode soon, blowing half the restaurant to rubble, making it impossible for firemen to enter and save the people slated to die. She turned away from the madness and broke another window with one mighty heave of the nearest chair, determined to make a difference in the fire's tragic outcome. Somehow.

But in the time it took her to break the window, flames had raced across the ceiling and begun to lick at the wall between her and the front door. The carpet of flames dancing across the ceiling rained debris down like rocketing meteorites. There was no one in this part of the restaurant now—they were all still trying to squeeze out the door in front. But she knew they were stuck...had foreseen the massive timbers and other debris that would block the exit after only a scant few managed to rush through the doors. With much disgust, Luna now doubted that anyone would escape through the windows as she had hoped they might.

Damn it. She hadn't come this far to give up now. She skirted past the hot flames and came up behind the crowd of people still trying futilely to get out, a mass of human bodies squirming and crushing others in an attempt to escape. "Come this way," she called shrilly. "There's a better way out."

Some people turned and Luna pointed to the broken windows. "You can still get out!"

The flames were now nearly blocking off the path to the windows, and Luna had to jump over some smaller ones snaking across the floor to get back. Three people followed her. Only three. They jumped out the windows, never looking back. Luna cast a worried glance behind her and saw that the entire restaurant was now being eaten by the fire. The exits she had made were now inaccessible.

She wanted to do something, anything, to save the others. But nothing had gone her way, not from the beginning. Luna eyed the flames, wondering if she could get through them to the people still swarming at the front of the restaurant. But the flames were hot and hungry, eating everything in their path with a voracious appetite.

Which meant no one could pass through from the other side. Luna had done all she could. Tears choking her, blurring her vision, she climbed out the window and escaped at the same moment the CO_2 tanks chose to explode.

It felt as if a giant, hot fist struck her brutally in the back. Luna was flung to the ground by the force of the explosion. Her cheek hit a rock and bled, but Luna didn't even pause over the tiny pain. She got to her feet, swayed dangerously, and looked at the restaurant as the fire raged through it unchecked. She saw that a fire truck had arrived, as well as a police car. Still, no one was rushing into the building. Luna knew it was assumed—thanks to a foolish waiter with a big mouth—that everyone had gotten out.

She ran to one of the firemen. "There are still people in there!" she screamed at him.

The man's eyes went wide with shock. He turned to one of his fellow firemen and spoke hurriedly. The fireman got an axe from the truck and hastened to chop through the timbers that had fallen and blocked the entrance while his brothers rallied to aid him, but it was not an easy job. So much debris had fallen. A massive barrier stood between rescue and death.

Spectators watched as the building burned. Covered in soot and smelling of smoke, Luna wandered among them, waiting to see if her efforts had been in vain. The firemen had at last forced their way through the debris and one lone fireman entered, coming out with a woman in his arms. More firemen went inside to retrieve more people, and the suspense nearly killed Luna.

In the end, only four people were pulled from the fire—people who would have survived even if Luna hadn't been there, she knew.

However, the ten—those important ten—remained inside, dead from smoke inhalation or burnt to death. Luna didn't have to be told that she'd failed. She knew the moment when most of the people within died. She knew it as certainly as she'd known the fire would begin.

Unable to bear it, Luna left the crowd and began to walk the several blocks back to Pulse's hotel. She held her hands crossed over her tummy, hugging herself protectively, and lurched dizzily as she walked. Her entire body hurt but it wasn't a physical pain. It was an emotional one, one she couldn't control or ignore. Without warning, she threw up, emptying the contents of her stomach on the dirty ground in a most inelegant way.

Tears were leaking freely out of her eyes now and though she tried to tell herself it was because the smoke had irritated them, she knew better. The horrible pain in her heart was back, crippling her. She cried quietly, stumbling on the cracked sidewalk, ignoring the few stares she earned from passersby.

It took her the better part of an hour to get back to the hotel. By then all her tears had been spent, or at least Luna hoped they had been. Her eyes were stinging and swollen and she knew she must look a fright.

Which was why she wasn't surprised when she was denied entrance into the hotel by the bellhop. She didn't possess any proof that she was a guest in the hotel. Luna thought to give him Pulse's name but realized that she didn't know his last name, or even if Pulse had used his real name to purchase the room in the first place. After trying unsuccessfully to gain entrance, Luna walked past the hotel and sat with her back against the brick wall of a neighboring building. She would wait until dark and hope that she could eventually get into the hotel once the shift changed.

Several hours passed. Luna stayed put, her mind a quandary of thoughts, ignoring the pain in her butt and back as she rested against the hard stone. Some people threw money to her as they passed, mistaking her for a vagrant as she simply sat there and stared off into space, unresponsive when anyone acknowledged her.

Her failure and her pain were absolute. All hope and happiness within her had fled, leaving a gaping hole in her soul that she had no hope of mending.

Dusk finally came, the sun dimming, turning the world into myriad strange, bluish colors. Luna rose from her position and tried once more to gain entrance to the hotel. Once again the same bellhop stopped her. But at the last moment, before she turned away again, she caught sight of Pulse in the lobby and breathed a heartfelt sigh of relief.

"Pulse," she cried out, voice hoarse from the smoke she had breathed, the screams she had raised in the restaurant and from her broken sobs at her resulting failure.

His dark head turned and his eyes found hers. He stalked to the entrance, looking ready to murder her.

She'd never been so happy to see anyone in her life.

"Where were you? I waited all day —"

"They wouldn't let me into the hotel," she explained, breaking into his surly greeting, feeling a lone, solitary tear slip down her cheek.

Pulse immediately turned on the bellhop that waited at the curb for arriving guests. "Why did you not allow entrance to this woman?" he demanded regally.

The bellhop sputtered, obviously more than a little nervous, dwarfed as he was by the giant Pulse. "I-I'm sorry, sir," he said, instantly recognizing the nearly seven-foot giant. "I d-didn't know she was with you," he explained, looking cornered and quite uncomfortable.

"Well, she is. Make a note of it, and do not interfere with her again."

Pulse took her hand and led her back into the hotel. He approached the desk and gave his name. Then he proceeded to add Luna's name to his room and request that she be given a key. The front desk clerk did as he wished, never once meeting Luna's eyes. And that was fine with her. She knew it was because of how atrocious she looked.

"Can I park my car here?" she asked quietly, subdued.

"It's fifty dollars a night," the desk clerk answered briskly.

Luna's eyes bulged. "Uh, never mind."

"We will bring the car around shortly," Pulse told the clerk.

"I can't afford that," she whispered to him, appalled.

"I can," he said simply. "Besides, your vehicle will be safer here, will it not?" He turned and directed the question to the desk clerk. The clerk nodded her head in answer, still refusing to meet Luna's gaze.

"Come." Pulse tugged on her hand. "You need a shower."

Luna went docilely enough. They called the elevator and waited silently for it to arrive. Once it did, they stepped inside, alone at last.

"How did it go?" he asked, reaching out and gently touching the cut on her cheek.

Luna hadn't thought she had tears left to shed, but hearing Pulse ask about her mission brought back all the pain and torment she'd fought so hard to subdue during the day. She began to shake and tears fell hot and fast down her cheeks.

"It didn't work. Ten people died," she said softly. "Ten. Just like I knew they would."

Pulse pulled her against him and embraced her, despite her obvious stiffness. He suspected she was used to comforting herself. "You tried. That is what is most important."

"After what happened with you, I thought maybe my luck had changed. That I could finally make a difference." Her breath sobbed brokenly out of her body. "It's this damned Cassandra Syndrome. It's run in the women of my family forever. No one will ever believe our predictions, and we'll never be able to change the outcome of the tragedies we're forced to envision. I hate it!"

"It's okay," he soothed, rubbing his hands up and down her back.

"No one listened to me. I pulled the fire alarm and everybody just sat there and looked around stupidly. I screamed 'fire', I made an absolute ass out of myself, but no one listened. No matter how hard I tried, I still wasn't able to change things."

"Did you ever think that if you hadn't been there, more people would have died? Have you ever wondered if maybe you are simply a tool of fate—that your premonitions are simply there to *induce* you to try and change things? That you are making a difference despite that it may seem like you are not?"

Luna sniffed. She wanted to believe his words, she truly did. "I did get three people out the window." Her face scrunched up. "No. Nothing I do matters. Those people would have lived without my help."

"You cannot carry this weight alone. You are not responsible for the world or the atrocities within it, whether you see them before they happen or not," Pulse said softly, his breath ruffling her hair. "You are a warrior, fighting a war that you cannot win."

She nodded against him then groaned. "Oh, who am I kidding?" she wailed, feeling empty but for the endless pain in her heart. "I can't let you console me. All those people died and I couldn't do anything to stop it. I really thought things would change, because of what you and I did with my last two premonitions. But nothing has changed. Nothing at all."

"You'll feel better after a shower," Pulse murmured as the elevator doors opened. He took her hand once more in his and led her down the corridor that would take them to his room.

When they were safely inside, Pulse guided her to the bathroom. Without asking her permission, he pulled her shirt from her and tossed it on the floor. His hands went to the fastening of her jeans and she tried to brush them away, blushing to the roots of her hair. But he was firm. He undid the clasp of her fly and pushed her jeans down around her ankles.

Luna stepped from the jeans, knowing Pulse wouldn't give up now that he'd started. He turned her around and worked on the fastenings of her bra. It took a long time, as if he were unfamiliar with the task, but finally he removed the bra and turned her again, baring her breasts to the air and to his gaze.

He stepped back and looked at her. Luna crossed her hands over her breasts and stood there, more than aware of the sudden static electricity in the room. The look of hot, unadulterated passion in his eyes made her cheeks burn. She grew breathless. Her nipples hardened deliciously beneath her hands and a warm ache spread from her breasts to her pussy, making her knees week with desire.

The tension in the air between them could have been cut with a knife.

Pulse dragged his gaze away from her body and he turned the shower on, checking the temperature of the water for her before nodding his approval. He took her hand and helped her into the shower, like a gallant knight of old, only far sexier, pulling the curtain closed with slow deliberation.

She heard Pulse leave the room, closing the door with a click behind him. Free now from his superheated, overwhelming presence, she settled herself beneath the spray. It wasn't as hot as she liked, so she cranked the knob up and waited for the water to warm her, shivering and crying silently.

Finally, Luna relaxed and let the water wash away the last of her tears.

Chapter Seven

೭౨

Luna belted the white hotel robe around her waist and exited the bathroom. She found Pulse sitting back against the pillows on the bed, pressing button after button on the remote control to the television. She hopped on the bed next to him and reached for the remote.

"It's easy once you get the hang of it." She showed him, changing the channels slowly.

"What is that box?" he asked, though he didn't sound too interested. Luna assumed he was merely trying to engage in idle conversation.

"It's a TV," she answered with a smile. "Are you saying you've never seen a television before? Everybody has one—you can't walk down the street without seeing one through a window."

Pulse eyed her, taking in the sight of her in the too-large terrycloth robe. "I haven't been up to the surface in over fifty years. What tee-vees I saw then looked nothing like this."

Luna choked on her surprise. "Fifty years?" she croaked. Well, she had to admit, conversations like this could distract anyone from even the worst of days.

Pulse nodded.

"How old are you?" she asked, incredulous. He looked no more than thirty, despite the silver in his hair.

"I'm am four hundred and nine...I think." He shrugged. "I'm not sure anymore."

"Holy moly! That's frickin' unbelievable. Do all Shikars live as long as you have?"

"We live until we are ready to go to the land beyond. Some of us choose to walk that path to the next life early on, after only a couple hundred years or so. But others, like myself, hang on to our life and to our duty. I haven't finished my work here yet. I won't go to the land beyond for many more years."

"Why don't you look older?" she asked curiously, reaching out despite herself and tracing a fine line of silver in his dark hair.

"We Shikars stop aging at around thirty or forty years of life. We do not grow old as your people do. I'm not exactly sure why."

"That is the most amazing thing I think I've ever heard," she told him with wide eyes. "I wish it were the same for us humans."

Luna looked back at the television and continued to change channels until she at last found Cartoon Network. *Foster's Home for Imaginary Friends* was playing—a show she hadn't seen in over a year but still remembered fondly. She settled back against the pillows at Pulse's side, watching the colorful cartoon spring to life on the screen.

"I need to get some clothes out of my car," she said idly, toying with the belt of her robe.

"I can go and retrieve the vehicle for you. I'll bring it here, if you like, and bring you a change of clothing too. That way you don't have to put your dirty clothes back on."

"I don't know," she said warily. "You didn't even know what a TV was, how can you know how to drive my car?"

"I have studied the mechanics of your vehicles for many years. It is a fascinating subject. Each year something new comes along to challenge me, but I am fairly certain I understand the basic principles. I'm not completely unaware of the advances of humankind, I just...choose what advances to learn of." A corner of his mouth lifted, and Luna found herself smiling back.

Luna laughed. "All right," she drawled, "you can try. It's an automatic so you shouldn't have *too* much of a problem." She got up and went to the bathroom, rooting around in her jeans pockets for her keys. Grabbing them from her front left pocket, she took them to Pulse and once more settled on the bed beside him. "Just keep an eye out for cops, okay?"

Pulse nodded, drawing her eye as he gently placed her keys on the bedside table. His gaze met hers and every dry hair on her body stood at attention. He moved slowly, giving her plenty of time to protest, at last placing his mouth on hers with gentle, seductive pressure.

Luna rose to her knees on the mattress, leaned close to Pulse and took his head in her hands, slanting her mouth on his, opening her mouth and giving him her tongue, taking control. The intent of his caress changed from soothing to enflaming. Desire swamped them both, drowning them under a monstrous wave of feeling that neither could control.

Pulse clutched her close, pulling her tight against him, filling her with the hum of his power. She felt the hard press of his phallus against her tummy and gasped into his mouth. With bold and eager hands she reached for him, stroking him through the barrier of his clothing. He groaned into her mouth and she swallowed the sound hungrily, pumping him gently up and down until he grew even thicker, even harder beneath her caress.

He was a big man. All over. That was more than evident by the shocking weight of his cock in her hands, even clothed as it was.

As she stroked him, Pulse's hands went to the fastening of her robe. He made short work of the knot in the belt and opened the flaps of terrycloth, revealing her nude body to his hungry gaze. One of his hands moved up to cup the weight of her naked breast, his thumb brushing over the hard, aching nipple so that she gasped and tightened her hold on him. Pulse's answering gasp brought a smile to her heart—her lips were otherwise engaged.

His hands pushed the robe from her shoulders then gently caressed each inch of flesh bared to him. When she was totally nude, he pulled her to him once again, crushing her breasts to his still clothed chest, and ran his hands down her back, all the way to her bottom.

Pulse stroked her ass, eliciting a broken cry from her lips. Heretofore she'd never noticed how sensual it felt to have one's bottom seen to, but now she knew that she loved it when a man played with her ass. He dug his fingers into the full globes and lifted them, separating them so that the air tickled even her most private parts.

They were both on their knees now. He lifted her with his hands beneath her bottom, bringing her nipple straight to his waiting mouth. The feel of his lips on her was like being struck by a bolt of lightning. Her entire body shook as he suckled her, holding her captive, tonguing and nibbling her nipple until she was moving her hips against his in an unmistakable invitation.

Her hands went between them, to the ties of his soft trousers. With shaking fingers, she undid the knot and was rewarded when the hot, thick length of him sprang forth, free and eager for her caress. His cock was smooth, velveteen, with a core of steel. Luna wrapped her fingers around him as best she could—he was so thick!—and stroked him carefully from base to tip, over and over again.

"Oh, Luna," he groaned against her breast. "Don't stop."

She had no intention of stopping. Indeed, she was fascinated by the feel of him in her hand, caught up in a web of desire she had no thoughts of escaping. Luna tightened her hold around him, reveling in the power she had over him as he gasped against her nipple with each wicked movement of her clever fingers.

Luna pushed his hands away from her and forced him to lie back with a palm to his chest. He did as she wanted, settling back amongst the pillows on the bed. It wasn't easy, but she pulled his pants down and off, throwing them behind her negligently. Bending over him so that her hair tickled over his heated skin, she took him in her mouth.

Pulse almost came up off the bed. He roared as she took him deep into the back of her throat, and fisted his hands in her wet hair. The flavor of him was wild on her tongue, fascinating her, intoxicating her. Her head bobbed up and down as she swallowed him over and over again, and he tightened his fingers in her hair.

Darting out her tongue, she licked him from tip to base and back. She flicked her tongue over the crown of his cock, satisfied when she felt him shiver beneath her. The taste of him in her mouth was wild and untamed. His flavor filled her head like a drug, making her want more and more and more.

Cupping his sac in her hand tenderly, she drove him wild with her mouth. There was no part of him she left undiscovered, no secrets that she left hidden. In that moment he was hers in all ways and she reveled in that knowledge.

His hands roved over her back and hair, tangling in the long locks. The sensation of his touch lit through her like electricity, making her body hum with pleasure. Indeed, with every caress, a mild shock raced through her, reminding her vividly that this was no mere human she was seducing.

Pulse pulled her off him, insisting when she tried to keep her mouth on his cock. He lifted her high against him and rolled them, shrugging off his tunic before he came to rest on top of her tingling body. Their naked skin touched from chest to feet, hot and smooth and wicked, sliding sensually each time they moved.

His fingers sought out and found the soft, curly hair of her sex. He stroked her like he might a cat and she fairly purred beneath his caress. Luna spread her legs wide to accommodate him, welcoming more of his wondrous touch. His fingers slipped into her wetness then and found her clit, swollen and aching and moist. He stroked it in little circles, making her come up off the bed with a wild cry as starbursts of color filled her body with vibrations she'd never before experienced.

The pad of his index finger pressed against her clitoris, exerting pressure slowly and by degrees. He slipped in her wetness but promptly returned, fingertip rough and hot against her silken flesh. Luna came with a broken cry, clutching him to her in desperation. Her only anchor in the storm of feeling that roared through her.

"What did you see?" he asked.

"I saw...light. Electric starlight," she said breathlessly.

He slipped one finger deep inside her. She felt her body stretch to accommodate him, swallowing him into her. His thumb pressed against her clit, moving in tiny, imperceptible circles. Luna gasped and closed her legs reflexively. Pulse slid down her body and pushed her legs apart, wedging his shoulders between her thighs so she couldn't close them again.

She was open before him, utterly. His gaze burned her wherever it roved, like a physical caress that was inescapable. Every touch of his skin on hers resulted in a mind-blowing shock. Slipping another finger into her, stretching her farther so that pain mingled with the pleasure, he pressed her clit firmly and she came once more.

Luna felt her body clench his fingers hungrily, swallowing him deep. Little flutters of ecstasy danced through her, robbing her of all rational thought. This time she saw blackness, interlaced with tiny pinpoints of light. With a long, low moan, she undulated on his hand, rolling her hips sensually, taking his fingers even deeper within her.

A third finger entered her and she felt impossibly tight around his hot, questing flesh. He thrust deep inside her, filling her, stretching her. She felt herself grow impossibly wetter, almost to the point of dripping onto the mattress. His fingers, their way eased by her juices, thrust in and out of her slowly, seductively.

He pressed her clit and she came again, immediately. He waited until she came down before twisting his fingers in her, stealing her breath once more. Panting, she bucked her hips, feeling him so deep and tight inside her that she was mindless to all else but the need to come. Over and over again.

When the tip of his tongue touched her it was as if she'd been set alight by fire. She let loose a little scream and arched up to receive more of his kiss. He removed his fingers and licked her from clit to anus and back, making her scream again. He thrust his fingers back inside her and pressed her clit hard with his tongue and she came with a violence that stunned her. He played her body like he would a fine instrument, calling forth sensations she'd never experienced, drinking down every response he wrought forth from her quivering, aching body.

"Oh god," she cried out, panting. "*Oh my god!*"

Pulse's fingers came out of her body with a wet sucking sound that enflamed both their senses. He came up over her body, pressing kisses all over her, especially on her belly and breasts. Taking her nipple deep into his mouth he sucked hard, eliciting another gasp and moan from her trembling lips.

With a moist, popping sound he released her and grabbed her legs, guiding them around his waist. He positioned himself at her portal, the great plum-shaped crown slipping inside her wetness. He rubbed himself against her, stroking her entire sex with his hot, velveteen cock. Luna writhed beneath him, begging to be taken.

"Please, Pulse. *Please*," she cried, head thrashing about on the pillow until her hair was a wild tangle about her.

Pulse bent his head and breathed into her mouth, filling her with his essence. "Do you want me?" he asked softly.

"Yes!" she cried, clutching him closer, her feet pressing into the small of his back. "I want you *sooooo bad!*"

"I've wanted you since the first moment I saw you," he admitted in a soft, gentle voice that belied his undeniable passion, taking his cock in his hand, guiding it into her.

The thick, smooth head of his cock slipped into her, stretching her wide. Her body yawned around his, welcoming him deeper within, and he slid, inch by delicious inch into her wet warmth. Luna had a moment of fear when she realized just how big he was. But the fear was forgotten, replaced by pleasure as he filled her.

When he was seated to the hilt, Luna felt sure she could feel him in the back of her throat, he was so large. Never in her life had she felt so fragile, so small. Her body was full of his cock—hot and heavy inside her—and weeping wetly for more. His hands rubbed over every inch of her skin, caressing her from head to foot. Soon she hummed with his power, relaxing beneath the claim of his demanding body.

The moment he felt her relax around him, he started to move within her. With graceful motions he rocked on top of her, undulating his hips into hers. Each slide of his velveteen flesh inside her wrung a cry from her lips. Breathless and weak from all her climaxes, she held on tight as he rode her into the stars yet again.

Waves of sensation crashed into her, drowning her. He stretched her so tightly, over and over, that tears began to leak from the corners of her eyes. The pleasure was so exquisite. She moaned again and again, beyond speech. Her body bucked against his, swallowing him deeper. His fingers reached down and pressed on her hard, aching clit, making her come yet again.

When she came down from her high, he was moving faster within her. But he was nowhere close to being done. He sought out her lips with his and thrust his tongue deep into her mouth, sliding alongside hers. His fingers found her stabbing nipples and squeezed them playfully. All the while he rode her and she was mindless to all but the needs of her body and his.

Luna tangled her hands in his silken hair. It fell around them like a dark curtain, locking out the rest of the world. Every breath she took tasted and smelled like him, making her dizzy. Making her crazed with need. Sweat broke out on her body so that they slid more easily against each other, and her heart beat a fast tattoo in her breast, throbbing through her and into him.

They were both fighting for breath. Luna was trembling so violently beneath him she felt sure she'd shake him off, but he held fast, still thrusting his hips into hers.

The smell of ozone suddenly filled her nose and the hairs on her body stood on end. The humming feel of his power washed through her, filling her up, ravaging her senses. Goose pimples broke out on her flesh. Luna clenched her teeth around a cry and held on tight to his broad shoulders, moving her hips beneath him.

After long, endless moments, he began to move even faster within her. Each thick delicious inch of him was hers and she reveled in that carnal knowledge. She claimed him as completely as he now claimed her, and Luna was proud to know that he was hers in that moment. Tightening her legs around his waist, she matched his pace, eliciting a deep groan from his lips.

Disbelievingly, she felt her body reach for another climax. Straining beneath him, she cried out and trembled as ecstasy once more filled her being. His talented fingers rubbed circles around her clit, wrenching another cry from her parched lips. Her pussy milked him with wild tremors, squeezing him tight, swallowing him whole.

Pulse gave a loud shout and surged into her. She had a moment of some intense feeling, like electricity arcing into her from his cock, deep inside her pussy. With another cry, he tore himself from her. She felt the hot splash of his cum hitting her belly as he spent himself outside her.

Luna was exhausted. She relaxed into the bed, boneless, panting hard, the sweat cooling on her body. Pulse came down to lay beside her, his fingers still idly toying with her nipple as he, too, fought for breath. A drop of sweat ran down his forehead and she licked it away, enjoying the salty flavor.

With such gentle care that tears teased the rims of her eyes, Pulse gently wiped away the traces of his cum from her skin with the soft, absorbent cloth of her discarded robe. He kissed her, a soft press of his mouth on hers that tasted of their sex and their repletion, and tossed the robe negligently over his shoulder.

Without a word, Pulse rose and dressed. Naked and unashamed, she simply reclined there and rallied the strength she would need to go into the bathroom and wash off. His eyes met hers, a storm brewing within them that she couldn't name. He grabbed her car keys off the bedside table, looked her over from head to toe as if he couldn't stop himself, and disappeared.

Chapter Eight

ဢ

Pulse climbed into Luna's car and shut the door. He laid his hands on the steering wheel and sighed heavily.

Something had happened back there in Luna's welcoming arms. He hadn't just had sex with her—he had made love to her. But it was even more than that. So much more. It was as if they'd possessed each other entirely, becoming one being, one soul. He'd never felt anything like it.

He'd had many women over the years, both Shikar and human. But he'd never reacted the way he just had with Luna. He hadn't even used protection, a violation of the very rules he fought so hard to enforce on his own warriors. True, he had been able, at the last moment, to pull free of her and spend himself on her smooth, silken stomach. But he had placed her in very grave danger with his actions, and he knew it.

Even stranger was the fact that he didn't care. Of course he cared that there was a risk to her. But he knew she was a strong psychic, more than capable of enduring the transformation from human to Shikar that his seed would cause. If only he could claim the power of her love.

Did he want her love? Absolutely. Was he ready to give her his...he wasn't certain. And he was *never* uncertain. About anything.

Luna had shaken him to the core. He hadn't expected that. She had given herself to him with a free enthusiasm that undid him. She had held nothing back—he'd seen to

102

that, wringing every response he could from her trembling flesh. He'd had to struggle mightily to keep a piece of himself from her, but he was beginning to think his struggles had been in vain.

She had touched his heart.

Pulse knew it was only a matter of time before he truly claimed her—made her his mate, made her a Shikar. It had been inevitable the moment she had spoken to him, he just hadn't fully realized it until now. The thought of her with another man, any man, drove him to the point of madness. No. He could no longer exist without her by his side.

He remembered her prediction that she would die, and soon. With a growl, he fought the thought away, unable to bear the idea of her in any danger. So she was supposed to freeze to death? Pulse would see to it that she was always warm, always safe. He vowed it then and there. If he had been able to change her predictions twice now, surely he could do it again by saving her life.

Putting the key in the ignition, he cranked the car to roaring life. He carefully put the vehicle in drive and pulled out of the parking space.

He could still smell her, on his hands, on his body. She smelled of flowers and tears and hope. It was an intoxicating fragrance and he knew it was her natural smell. No perfume could have compared.

And the taste of her! Wonderful. Exquisite. He already wanted more of her exotic flavor on his tongue. He wanted to lick her pussy until she came a hundred times over. He wanted to feel the trembling of her wet flesh, wanted to feel her come around his tongue and lips. He was already hard once more just thinking about it and he wondered when she would be up for another romp in the bed. He knew he had ridden her hard, pulling every climax he could from her lithe body, and it would take a little time for her to recuperate. Not too long, he hoped.

He sighed and carefully maneuvered the car in the heavy New York traffic.

A strange, all too familiar feeling washed through him. His skin felt stretched tight over his bones and it seemed as if a two-ton weight was pressing onto his chest.

Daemons. They were close. He could feel them.

Here? In New York City, the bustling capital of American accomplishment? There were millions of people around, endless bright lights illuminating almost every street. The Daemons were brave indeed to enter such an environment. Or very desperate.

In a panicked hurry now, he darted in and out of the lanes, progressing closer to the hotel. He knew that Luna was the Daemons' target. Who else could be such a powerful lure for their voracious appetites? Luna was the strongest woman he'd ever met—such strength would be impossible for the monsters to resist. And he knew his own presence would mark her, lure the monsters like moths to a flame.

He arrived at the hotel and jumped out of the car. The valet moved to claim the vehicle but Pulse shook his head. "Keep it running. I'll be back in a moment." He reached into the backseat and rummaged until he found some suitable clothes for her to wear and ran into the hotel, uncaring of the stares he drew as he passed, concerned only with his woman's safety.

* * * * *

Luna was wrapped loosely in the bed sheet when he entered, once again watching cartoons. "I called the police and let them know about the robbery tonight," she said in greeting. "I had to get the number from directory assistance, though, so you'll be charged for two calls."

He ignored her words. "Put these on, love. Quickly," he said, throwing the clothes to her.

Luna heard the underlying worry in his tone and reacted instantly. "What's wrong?"

"Daemons. Close. We have to leave this place. We can ill afford an incident, especially among so many humans. I have to get you out of here."

Luna dressed faster than she ever had in her life. "Are you sure?" she asked, pulling her shirt down over her head.

"Yes. Hurry now." Pulse gathered their things together and reached for her just as she finished putting her tennis shoes on. He grabbed her hand and his case of belongings and made for the door.

Luna had to run to keep up with him. "Where are we going?"

"Anywhere but here," he said shortly as they entered the elevator. More than anything he wanted to simply Travel with her, take her to his home where he knew she would be safe, but he knew he had to first lead the Daemons away from the bustling city and destroy them if he could. It was his duty, and his feelings for this woman — though just as important — must not sway him from his course.

They were silent as the elevator slowly brought them to the ground floor, both of them tense with the waiting. They bolted from the elevator once it reached the lobby, running out to her car which was waiting for them on the curb.

Luna jumped into the driver's seat, waited for Pulse to throw his bag in the back before climbing in beside her, and pulled out into the thick traffic. They were quiet as she concentrated on the road, pulling in and out of lanes in a way she would have never dared before, eliciting several horn blows for her efforts.

Tense, long minutes passed as they gradually made their way out of the city proper. It seemed to take an eternity but traffic eventually thinned and Luna made her way onto the interstate at last. Some of the feeling of urgency dissipated as she increased her speed on the open road, and she let out a sigh of relief.

"I was going to go see how the cops reacted to my tip," she said. "That's about fifty miles from here. Is that far enough, do you think?"

"It will have to do for now. But I do not think it is wise to linger in any one place for long."

"Why?"

"Because it will lure more Daemons to us."

Luna choked. "You mean they're *tracking* us? How?"

"They are sensing your power. And mine. Together, we are too tantalizing for the Daemons to resist. They will be on our heels from here on out. Now that they have found us, they will not let us go so easily."

"But I haven't seen a Daemon in years. Why would they sense me now?"

"They have sensed you from the beginning. That is why you saw them in your youth—you and your mother had such power and they coveted that for themselves. It is a miracle neither of you were killed by the beasts." He took a deep, calming breath and slowed his rushed words. "I think the Daemons have been unable to keep up with you as you travel from city to city, since your power is dormant for a time after each relocation. They haven't been able to pinpoint your location. That is why you haven't seen them in recent years. But they have been hunting you all the same, doubt it not. Their appetites are endless."

"You know how to kill them?" she asked with little worry in her voice.

He looked at her as if she were crazy. "Of course. I have been battling the Daemon Horde for centuries."

Luna grinned at him, helpless not to in her relief. "Then I'm not worried. I know you'll take care of me."

"Damn it, woman, do not play with your life so. This is a very dangerous situation."

"Oh, I'm sure it is. But you have to remember—I won't die. And I haven't had any visions that say you will either. So don't worry. If the monsters do find us then we'll just kill them and move on. No problemo."

Pulse ran a hand through his hair in agitation. "I have never met someone as nonchalant as you are about our enemies. How *can* you be—you have seen them. You know what they are capable of. By your own admission you have tried to kill them, and even succeeded once. How can you not be afraid?"

"Lighten up, Pulse. I didn't say I wasn't scared. I am a little, of course I am. But I told you, we'll be fine. I know it. So you don't have to worry."

Pulse sat back against the seat and looked out the window. "When did you first know you were going to die?" he asked softly, as if he had to know the answer.

"Well, I've known it since birth, duh." she laughed. "But I didn't know how. I finally knew I would freeze to death about two months ago, when I was in Michigan. I left because I was scared a snowstorm would come and take me, but I calmed down once I reached New York."

"Why?" He turned to look at her.

Luna shrugged and glanced his way. "I don't know. I guess I came to terms with the inevitable. I haven't been able to change the outcome of my premonitions—not until you arrived in my life. I knew I couldn't change the outcome of my fate, so I stopped worrying. Plus, I'll probably head farther south when it get cooler here."

"And you've grown careless with your own life since."

She frowned, not liking how he'd phrased his accusation. "Not really."

"Yes, really," he insisted. "You walk out into traffic without even looking. You put yourself in a burning building without a second thought. You live in your car."

"Hey. I lived in my car long before I saw my own death, thank you very much." She snorted.

"You are too impulsive. I do not know how you have survived this long without me to keep you in check."

"Yeah, well, that's just one of life's great mysteries," she drawled scathingly. "Look, I know what I'm doing. You don't have to worry about me."

"You're gambling with your life."

"No, I'm not. I told you, I saw how I die. There's nothing to be concerned about," she said in mounting exasperation.

Pulse growled and ran his hand through his hair once more, giving it a wild, disheveled look.

Luna peeked at him from the corner of her eye. "So. How was it?"

"How was what?" he frowned.

"Sex. With me." She giggled then quickly stifled the sound, embarrassed by it. "How was it?"

Pulse looked like he would choke for a moment, then laughter escaped his lips, surprising them both. "You are too much, love," he said between chuckles. "I cannot possibly keep up."

Luna waited for him to continue, then realized that he didn't mean to. "Well?" she prodded, impatient with his lingering silence.

"You know you were magnificent," he said dryly, but there was a thick, unmistakable flame of desire in his voice.

"Yeah. You weren't too bad yourself," she responded with a cheeky grin.

"I'm the best you've ever had," he said arrogantly.

Luna laughed again, and the last of the day's worries and disappointments left her. "Yes. I won't lie. You *are* the best. No one could compare."

Pulse looked satisfied with her answer and gazed out the window once more.

"So?" she prodded.

"So what?"

He infuriated her with his stubbornness. "So, was I the best *you've* ever had, or what?"

Pulse turned to her and put his hand on her thigh. His touch burned her through her jeans. "You were, by far, the most glorious thing I have ever seen, touched, smelled or tasted. There. Does that satisfy your endless curiosity?"

Luna laughed and put her hand on his, tangling their fingers together. "Yeah."

"Good. Now drive. You are making me crazy with all this chatter, woman. I am trying to think."

"Think about what?"

"About how we must proceed from here."

"Well, I was thinking I could pull over and we could have a quickie," she teased.

"For Grimm's sake, woman, I wasn't talking about sex! I was talking about the Daemons. We need to have a plan of action in case they attack."

Luna grinned. "You go ahead and think then. I'll just be over here until you're ready for that quickie."

Pulse growled and turned his head away once more, but not before Luna saw the spark of desire that lit his eyes and the crack of a smile that curved his lips.

Luna sighed contentedly and settled in for a long drive.

Chapter Nine

ᔥ

"Awesome. The cops are already here," she noted excitedly. "Finally, someone in law enforcement has listened to me." Luna watched the empty police cruiser, wondering if the sight of it would deter the would-be criminals. She hoped so. But she doubted it.

"I do not like it here. The area is too lightly guarded. There are too many open fields. We are mere targets here," Pulse said, looking about them alertly.

"Just be patient with me for a few minutes. I want to make sure the cops stay until the crooks show up," she said. Luna glanced at her watch, pressing a button on the side to illuminate the dial in the darkness. "Only seven more minutes, okay?"

"A lot can happen in seven minutes," Pulse pointed out stonily.

Luna was quiet for a long while, thinking. "There's going to be a plane crash in Philadelphia tonight," she said at last, softly.

"Will anyone be hurt?" he asked, his voice equally soft.

Luna nodded. "Yeah. Eight will die, but twelve will survive with only a few minor injuries."

"How does it happen? Can you see that?" he asked gently.

She cleared her throat nervously. Luna still wasn't used to sharing her predictions with anyone else. "One of the engines will catch fire because of an electrical defect missed by the technicians who checked the plane before

111

takeoff. It'll go down pretty fast, in a patch of woods just outside the city limits. Thank god it's just a small plane or more could die."

Pulse looked around them, glowing gaze piercing thorough the darkness to search for anything out of the ordinary. "How do you know these things? Do you have visions? Does the knowledge come to you? How does your gift work?"

Luna let out a whoosh of breath. "Well, it's like a switch goes off in my brain and I suddenly know, without any self-doubt, what is going to happen. I don't really have visions per se, though I do see some images in my mind when the realizations come. I just…know things. It's as though I've always known them, but have only just uncovered the memory. Does that make sense?"

"And you can predict things that will happen far away?"

"Yeah. Sometimes." Luna thought for a moment. "But most of the time I know about things that will happen close to me. It's almost like a torture device—my premonitions hit close to home, giving me the chance to try to change the outcome. I always take the chance, but I always fail. My predictions aren't very useful," she admitted sourly.

They were parked down the road from the bank, just able to see the patrol car out front. Luna glanced at her watch then looked back at the bank. She saw a dark figure emerge from the entrance and head towards the car. It was a lone police officer. He got into the car and cranked it up, and Luna cried out in protest.

"No!" Luna wailed. "Damn it, he only needs to stay a few more minutes! Why is he leaving—I told them the exact time to be here!"

The patrol car pulled out of its parking space and headed down the road away from them. Luna watched it, tears of frustration in her eyes, until the vehicle disappeared into the darkness. "No. No!" She pounded angrily on the steering wheel. "God, why are people so stupid?" she growled, unbuckling her seat belt and reaching for the handle of the door.

"What are you doing?" Pulse asked, more than a little concerned. "You are *not* about to leave this car."

"I have to go in. Maybe there's still something I can do to help." She got out of the car and stood beside it. Pulse got out as well and glared at her over the top of the station wagon.

"We have to be careful not to touch anything. My prints are on file and I don't want the police wondering what I was doing at a bank heist," Luna warned him absently, determined not to meet his fierce gaze.

They approached the bank cautiously, both looking around for any sign of a threat, human or otherwise. Nothing stirred in the night save the crickets and tree frogs, which made just enough racket, Luna thought, to mask the sound of a break-in. She glanced down at her watch nervously. "Only a couple minutes left," she told Pulse flatly. "Let's hurry."

They both ran up the steps that lead to the bank's entrance. Luna wasted no time, pounding on the door with her fist the moment she reached it. A long, tense moment passed. Nothing. Then, just when Luna was growing frantic, a security guard came to the window.

"Please, sir, you have to listen to me. There's going to be a break-in any minute, you need to get out!" Luna called to him through the glass.

Too late. An old Chevy Impala, tires screaming, came out of the night and slammed to a stop at the base of the steps. Luna turned towards it with a grimace. Two young hoods got out of the car and began to approach. They were holding crowbars in their hands, and Luna knew for a fact that one of them had a gun concealed in the back of his belt.

"Not tonight, boys," she told them in a loud voice, unafraid, worried only for the safety of the guards within the building. "There's no way you're getting in this bank tonight."

"Who the fuck are you?" one of the two men asked with an evil sneer.

Luna felt, rather than saw, the other man reach behind him for the gun. "I'm Luna," she answered simply, approaching them slowly.

Pulse put his hand on her shoulder and forcibly pulled her back.

"I don't know you," the man with the gun said. "I don't know either of you. Get out of my way or you're gonna get hurt." He leveled the weapon on them menacingly.

"Look. There are two guards inside. They won't let you in," Luna warned him desperately.

The man with the gun—Larry, she knew suddenly—laughed. "We don't need no one to let us in, bitch." He brandished his handgun gloatingly. "I got all the permission we need to enter right here."

"Larry," she said, trying a different tactic and relishing the look of shock on the man's face when she said his name. "You don't want to kill anybody tonight. And you don't want to *be* killed, either. Let it go. Tonight just isn't your night, okay?"

Larry fired the gun. Luna never flinched. She didn't get a chance to. In the split millisecond it took for the bullet to reach her, Pulse had thrust a blade in front of her and deflected it. Luna gasped, seeing that the three-foot blade had shot from his wrist, out over his hand, like an extension of the bone within. Tiny trails of electricity crawled up the blade, making eerie sparks in the darkness that crackled audibly.

Larry, clearly panicked now, fired the gun at Pulse. Once again Pulse deftly blocked, sparks flying both from the deflection of the bullet on the metal blade and the electricity that arced with the impact. Instantly the blade retracted back into Pulse's arm, and he then stalked down to the crook and punched him in the side of the head with his fist, knocking him out cold before the punk could think to fire again. Pulse then turned to the other man. "Leave," he said flatly, his voice a cold and fearful command.

The man nodded and stumbled backward. He got into the car, leaving his buddy behind on the steps, and sped away.

Pulse turned to Luna and she was amazed at the heated glow in the depths of his amazing eyes. Behind them, one of the security guards came through the glass door. "How the hell did you do that?" he asked, eyes wide on Pulse's hand as if he feared the blade might appear once more and do him harm.

Pulse approached him and put his hands on either side of the man's face. "You will forget what you have seen here," he said softly, so softly that Luna almost didn't hear him.

The man's face went blank and slack. Luna watched as he turned around smartly and went back into the bank without a backward glance.

"Neat," she laughed, so relieved she didn't even have words to express how she felt.

Pulse smiled at her and it was the most beautiful smile she'd ever seen.

"What was that thing?" she asked, motioning towards the hand that had sprouted the glowing, electric sword.

"It is a Foil. All Shikars have them," he explained, as if he were some sort of professor teaching a student.

"Cool," she marveled, her racing heart beginning to slow now that the danger was over. "Is it metal? It looked like metal."

"Not really. It's a mineral deposit, an extension of our bones that we can use as weapons in times of crises. Some of us—members of the Foil Master Caste—can even throw them."

"Awesome. I want some!"

"Are you okay?" he asked abruptly.

She blinked. "Yeah. Thanks to you."

His face grew serious. "Don't ever step in front of a man with a gun again. Okay?"

"Okay," she said docilely.

"Promise me," he commanded.

"Okay."

"If nothing else, do it so that I never have to see you in such danger again."

"Okay."

Pulse growled. "And stop saying okay."

Luna nodded. "Okay."

They stepped over the still unconscious Larry and went back to Luna's car. "*You* did it," she said, as it dawned on her what had just happened. "*You* changed things."

"We did it. Together. That is why it worked. We need each other's help in order to change the path that fate has set." Pulse sounded so certain of it.

Luna clapped her hands with uncontrollable excitement. "I can't believe it. This is just too cool. Now," she sobered. "What do we do next?"

"I don't know," Pulse admitted. "You're the one driving."

"Well, it's pretty obvious we'll need to find a place to stay before morning or you'll go all crispy on me. It's hours 'til daylight, so we still have time to find someplace down the road." They climbed into the car and Luna started the engine with a turn of the key.

Pulse settled in beside her as she pulled away from the bank. He thought quietly for a long time, before speaking softly. "I think I have a better idea."

"What's that?"

He knew his duty, knew too that the Daemons still posed a threat, one that he must eliminate. Yet he could not let his woman remain in danger one second longer. He wasn't strong enough to do that. "You can come with me, to my world. It is there that you will be safest," he said, studying her face for a reaction.

Luna laughed. She glanced his way and saw that he wasn't joking. She choked back the laughter abruptly. "You're serious."

"I am."

"But won't the other Shikars...I don't know, think it's weird that you're bringing a human into their midst?" she asked, still reeling from the very idea of seeing a new place, a new world.

"It is not as uncommon as you might think," he chuckled.

Laughing nervously, she tightened her hands on the steering wheel. "I don't know," she said hesitantly. "It would be really weird. And I'm sure that you're getting tired of me by now."

"You know I am not," he said stonily. "Don't be foolish. This is a good solution to our current problem. I can keep you beyond the reach of the Daemons. And there is the benefit that you can use your predictions to help us in our war."

Several miles passed and Luna thought hard on his words before coming to a decision. "I can't promise you anything. If I go with you, it may be weeks before I have another premonition. And even then I can't say if I would be of any use to you. I can't pick and choose when—or what—prediction will hit me next," she warned him.

"I am aware of this. I am willing to wait as long as it takes. I am certain you will be a valuable asset to my people."

"And what about you?" she whispered. "Will I be a valuable asset to *you*?" She both dreaded and anticipated his answer.

"You know I desire you, love. In my home we can explore each other at our leisure. There will be no one to interfere," he said gruffly, some unnamed emotion thick in his voice.

"I'm not worried about that." She gritted her teeth audibly. "I'm worried that once you're tired of me, I'll be stuck there. Alone. In a strange world. No. It's just too much. I can't do it." She shook her head, trying to rid herself of the wonderful, tempting thought of joining him in his world.

"I will *not* tire of you," he growled fiercely.

"You don't know that," she pointed out with forced practicality.

"I *do* know it," he snapped. "It is a fact. And you shall never tire of me—I will see to it. This is the perfect solution."

"No, it isn't," she said stubbornly.

"Give me a reason why. You have no home. No family or friends. You're alone here, cut adrift from the rest of humankind. I can give you a home and a safe haven from your worries and troubles. You won't ever again have to fear freezing to death," he added softly.

Luna thought quietly. "I don't know. I'm nervous." She admitted it freely, without shame. "I don't know what to expect."

"Neither do I. But it doesn't matter. So long as we are together, we can face any challenge. Haven't the past few nights taught you anything? We make a good team, you and I." He reached out and touched her cheek tenderly.

"But your mission," she pointed out. "You wanted to find something that would redeem mankind in your eyes. We haven't found that yet. We need more time."

"I have fulfilled my mission," he said softly. "I've seen everything I need. You have shown me, by your actions, that not all humans are a lost cause. You have redeemed your people, Luna. You alone. I will return to my post as an Elder. I will continue to work to save the human race from our enemies. The Council will be pleased and I will maintain my honor."

"You can't just decide all this, not in a few nights," she protested, though his words filled her with pride.

"I knew the minute I saw you step out into traffic to stop that vehicle that my mission was already complete. You braved the danger, selflessly and without hope of reward other than to save the life of that woman and her unborn child. You did not know her. You had never before met. Yet still, you fought to save her. How could I *not* see the good in you? And if there is good in you, I am certain there is good in others, though it might sometimes be difficult to remember."

"I don't know," she hesitated, still unsure.

"Come with me. Be with me. Together we are a formidable team. Together we can face the future with excitement and acceptance."

Luna sighed and pulled over into the emergency lane, ignoring the blaring of horns as cars whizzed past. She turned the car off and looked at him, her gaze tangling with his. "Have sex with me," she murmured. "Right here, right now. I don't have any doubts when I'm in your arms. Show me that you want me. *Make* me believe it."

Pulse didn't have to be told twice.

Chapter Ten

ಬ

"Take off your clothes. I want you naked in my arms," Pulse commanded with an arrogance that brought a tilt to her lips.

Luna shimmied out of her jeans. It was awkward, she had to push off her tennis shoes to get them past her ankles, but she soon had them off. She pulled her shirt over her head and threw it into the backseat. The only things that remained were her white lace bra, panties and socks.

"All of it," he said shortly, watching her with ravenous eyes.

Luna took off her underwear with trembling fingers and sat, completely nude, waiting to see what he would do next.

He reached for her, easily dragging her across the seat and into his lap. He guided her legs to either side of his thighs so that she straddled him, and he pressed tight to her to prove how much he wanted her. His cock was already hard and ready and she gasped as he lifted his hips slightly and rubbed it against her pussy through the fabric of his trousers.

"Is that for me?" she murmured with a smile.

"You know it is," he returned gruffly, pressing even tighter to her so that she gasped.

He pulled her close and captured her mouth with his. Her eyes fell closed and the hot, silken feel of his lips pressed against hers made her feel faint with excitement. That strange hum that was his power flowed through her like a river, shocking her skin to aching life. He put a hand on either side of her face, gently, tenderly. His thumbs pressed into the corners of her lips, opening them for the invasion of his tongue.

The taste of him poured into her mouth, filling her head with his flavor. She was dizzy, drunk on his exotic scent, and she clutched tight to him as a storm sparked to life within her. Her fingers dug into the flesh of his shoulders and she trembled against him with mounting excitement.

He suckled gently on her tongue, inviting her to explore inside his mouth. She ran her tongue along the ridge of his teeth, then delved deeper, greedily wanting more. Their breath mingled. Each time she gasped, he breathed into her, filling her with a delicious hum of power. Each time she made a noise he swallowed the sound and demanded more.

Luna darted her tongue out and licked his full lower lip delicately. His arms were about her waist, his hands rubbing her back softly, fingers tangling in the ends of her long hair as he toyed with the strands. She ran her hands over the ridge of his muscled chest, reveling in the feel of his strength through his clothes, kissing him for all she was worth.

His cool, silken hair tickled her face. Its scent, like the scent of his skin, had a combination of sweet and woodsy undertones. It made her dizzy. She put her hands in his hair and pushed it back behind his ears. She noticed he had slightly pointy ears and for some reason that made her giggle.

"What is it?" he growled against her mouth.

"Your ears are pointy." She giggled again.

Pulse ran a hand through his hair, hiding his ears with the dark strands before once more pulling her close against him. He kissed the side of her neck, nipping her with his teeth so that she gasped at the tiny pain before he laved it with his hot, wet tongue.

Her head fell back as he rained kisses on her throat, neck and shoulders. His hands came around her and palmed her breasts, squeezing them sensually. His thumbs flicked her nipples, bringing them to diamond hardness, making her writhe against him.

The hairs on her body stood on end and the air inside the car was thick with an electric charge. The smell of ozone filled her head until the scent of it mixed beautifully with Pulse's own natural aroma. Each time he touched her with his fingertips a tiny spark of electricity lit up the darkness and made her gasp.

Luna kissed his hair, his temple, his cheek, anything her lips could reach. He tasted salty and sweet at the same time, his flesh delicious and alluring. Her mouth was swollen and aching from his kisses, yet still she wanted more. She jerked his head up and slanted her lips on his, delving her tongue deep.

Pulse ran his fingers over her shoulders and down her arms, taking her wrists in his hands. He pulled her hands down slowly, until they rested benignly on her thighs. With a growl, he clutched her tighter to him, crushing her breasts against his cloth-covered chest, suckling hungrily on her tongue.

Impatient, Luna tugged at his tunic, pulling it up to expose the taut muscles of his stomach so that her hands could wander eagerly over his naked skin. He sucked in his breath at her light touch as she traced lazy circles over the six-pack of muscle he sported. She ran her hands under the tunic, enjoying the feel of him, delicately testing the strength of his large, smooth pecs.

The sound of her panting breaths echoed in the car, titillating them both, spurring on their desire to ever increasing heights. Pulse's hands left her and worked to remove his tunic. He made short work of it, tossing the clothing behind him negligently. Then he reached for her again and their bare chests touched, wringing a moan from her aching lips and a groan from his.

His skin was golden bronze, dark in the night. She ran her fingers over all that exquisite, naked flesh, trembling with desire. The bright glow of his eyes pierced the darkness, burning right to the heart of her, seeing into her soul. The demanding weight of his erection burned her through his clothing, making her so wet she was afraid she'd soak his pants.

Pulse lifted her with an easy strength, laying her shoulders and upper back against the dashboard carefully, opening her more fully to him. He ran his hands over her breasts, pinching and pulling her nipples until they were so hard they hurt. But the pain was delicious, mixing flawlessly with her passion. His hands left her breasts, the cool air causing them to tingle. The tips of his fingers trailed over her stomach and down, farther, until she was arching wantonly into his touch.

With one hand he held her thigh, keeping her still. With the other, he slid his fingers into the wet channel of her pussy. Luna cried out and bucked against his touch, seeing stars in the darkness. The shock of his fingers made her flesh sting and burn and ache for more. His power filled her, making her whole body hum with pleasure, making her flesh break out into goose bumps.

He rubbed her thigh gently, squeezing it delicately while he worked her pussy. His fingers slipped in her moisture and they both gasped at the intensity of her response to him. He found her clit easily and rubbed tiny circles around it with his thumb and forefinger, squeezing it so that it swelled, stealing her breath away. It was almost too much for her to bear.

Luna fought against the approaching climax. But Pulse would have none of her stubbornness. He stroked her wet cunt demandingly, forcibly pushing her up into the heavens.

She came with a tiny cry. Her head fell back, limp, hitting the windshield painfully but she didn't care. All she could feel was pleasure, pure and intense, unlike anything she'd ever felt before. The climax made her scalp hurt and her fingertips tingle. Her whole body felt swollen and full. Tremor after tremor shook her until she was quaking uncontrollably, mindless in her ecstasy.

His fingers had stilled on her while she came, but as she floated back down to earth he started to stroke her once again. He thrust his long middle finger into her, filling her so that she gasped. His thumb pressed on her clit and he thrust his finger into her over and over. Soon one finger became two, and she was stretched tight, full of him.

The hand on her thigh moved to cup her ass. He thrust hard into her, wringing a gasp from her lips. The hand at her ass shifted and he allowed his fingers to trace the seam of her bottom, before delving deeper to press against her anus. Pulse let his finger enter her to the first knuckle, making tears of mingled pleasure and pain leak from the corners of her eyes.

Luna was moaning uncontrollably. She thrashed her head about and strained against him, body hungry for another release. Her mind was devoid of all thought—only pure need filled her head and her senses. Pulse seemed to understand her body's desire and his thumb pressed her clit, rubbing it, squeezing it, until he pushed her to the edge once more.

"*Oh god*," she cried as she came a second time. "Oh, Pulse, that feels *soooo* good!"

She felt tremors as her pussy squeezed and released his fingers. Her ass trembled, bearing down on his finger, filling her with a decadent pleasure. Her body yawned for a deeper, fuller penetration. Once she had regained her breath, aftershocks still coursing through her, Luna's shaking hands went to the fastenings of his trousers. She fumbled with the tie, tangling it so that she groaned in frustration.

Pulse gently eased his finger out of her ass. He brushed her hands aside and untied the laces of his pants himself, freeing the thick length of his cock. Luna stared at it, wide eyed. He was so big—she'd never get over the shock of just how huge he was. She ate him with her eyes.

Grasping her hip with his hand, he guided her onto his cock, the purple, plum-shaped crown easing into her wetness. With his free hand he stroked her clit to aching hardness, easing his way deeper and deeper into her welcoming body. Luna leaned back, arching higher to receive him.

He filled her, inch by inch. One…three…six…nine inches, she felt them all the way to the back of her hoarse throat. Finally he was seated to the hilt, splitting her wide open. Pulse lifted her, bouncing her on him so that he could begin to thrust in and out of her throbbing cunt. Luna moaned breathlessly, her body taking his, swallowing him over and over.

The feel of him sliding into her was like wet silk on fire. It seemed as if she had a fist lodged inside her, filling her so completely that she didn't know where she stopped and he began.

Pulse was losing his tight grip on his control. The feel of her surrounding him, so wet and tight, stole his thoughts away. She was like fire in his arms, unpredictable and ever changing. She leaned back so far that her breasts pointed to the heavens. He bent his head and popped one of her thick, long, rosy nipples into his mouth, pounding himself into the heart of her.

The car was rocking with their motions, but Pulse did not care. He was a slave to her desires, to his desires. A bolt of lightning lit up the sky, striking only feet away from the car with a deafening crash.

She started violently. "What was that!?"

"It's all right," he said breathlessly around his mouth full of nipple. "I just got a little carried away."

Luna eased back once more, moving her hips over him like a dream, wringing a broken cry from his lips. He pounded harder into her, feeling an urgency overtake him that he could not control. The wet, sucking sounds her body made as he moved within her drove him wild, pushing him to the edge.

He wanted her to join him. Pulse sought out her clit—she was so sensitive there—and rubbed it roughly. Luna screamed and her body clamped down on his. Pulse groaned, feeling her body's tremors milking his cock.

He wanted it to last, wanted to bring her over a few more times. But his need drove him hard and he had no choice but to join her at the pinnacle of passion. At the last moment he remembered to pull out, and lifted Luna quickly to do so. His cum, white and pearlescent in the darkness, spurted forth from the thick crown of his sex. His seed spilled on his clothing, wetting the material, but it did not reach Luna. He was careful not to let it.

With a groan he leaned back against the seat heavily. He felt totally drained and yet strangely powerful at the same time. Breathing hard, he watched as she came down from her high, unable to keep his hands from roaming all over her delectable little body. He wanted to claim every inch of her for himself.

Luna was sure she would faint. Her body felt like the sun, full of all the heat and energy he had to give. Her entire being ached decadently. When she had enough breath with which to speak, she fell on him, clutching him tight.

"Oh, my god. Okay. Okay. You talked me into it," she said weakly.

"I knew you'd see reason," he chuckled.

"But you have to promise me if I want to come back here, you'll take me. I don't want to feel trapped," she cautioned.

"I promise. You never have to feel trapped, not with me."

Luna crawled from his lap and collapsed onto her own seat. She turned around and rooted in the back of her car for a moment before pulling a large, stuffed duffel bag into her lap. "Just a few essentials," she said. "Some clothes and soap and stuff." She handed the bag to him, motioning for him to put it on the floorboard at his feet.

"You won't need it. I can clothe you and I assure you, I have plenty of soap." He grinned, tucking the bag down by his feet.

"Yeah, well, I still want to bring mine. I don't want to leave everything behind, you know?" Luna turned to the backseat once more and grabbed a pair of panties, jeans and a soft, well-worn T-shirt. She also grabbed a roll of paper towels and gave it to Pulse, who used the sheets to dry the semen, still wet and glistening on his clothes.

Pulse finished and watched her as she awkwardly got dressed.

"I want to take the car to the ride-share parking lot and leave it there. It can stay a couple of weeks before anyone will think to tow it away. That'll give us plenty of time to come back and get everything from my car, should I choose to stay in your world," she told him, buckling her seat belt.

Luna cranked the car to life and pulled back onto the still busy interstate. It was a long time before either of them broke the silence.

When Luna at last pulled into the ride-share parking lot, Pulse looked about warily. He felt the faint presence of the Daemons, but that did not necessarily mean they were near enough to attack just yet. He knew they would circle inward, like a school of sharks, before they struck. That gave them some time.

Luna got out of the car and checked in all the windows to make sure nothing of value was peeking out to tempt would-be thieves. Pulse grabbed her duffel bag and got out. He came to her side and Luna locked the doors tight.

A savage roar rent the silence of the night.

Luna jumped. "Whoa. That Daemon sounds pissed."

Pulse looked into the darkness beyond the lights of the parking lot. He sighed. "I can't just let them stay up here. It is my duty to make sure they are destroyed."

Luna nodded. "I understand. I'll wait here while you go rout the bastard out."

Pulse turned and ran off in the direction he felt most certain the Daemons waited. Luna watched as he disappeared into the darkness before walking around to the passenger side to check the car one last time. Satisfied, she turned and leaned her back against the car and slowly sank down to the ground, weary to the bone. She sighed, delighting in the tight pull of her abused muscles.

She could still feel him inside her. Filling her. Stretching her. Making her come. She shivered delicately, though the air was far from chilly.

Several long minutes passed in silence. Just when she began to worry that Pulse had gotten lost, Luna saw a bolt of lightning arc through the sky in her peripheral vision, and heard a deafening explosion from behind the car.

She peeked up over the hood in the direction Pulse had taken.

Orange, pus-filled eyes stared at her, but feet away. Luna shrieked and stumbled backward, landing hard on her ass. The smell of the creature reached her then. It smelled like rotting flesh, sewage and brimstone, making her gag.

The creature jumped over the hood of the car, high into the air—several feet—and landed on the ground right in front of her. She rolled away as it reached for her with its jagged, foot-long claws, took to her feet and began to run. The creature leapt into the air once more, slamming to the ground directly in her path, shaking the earth and shattering the pavement into dust. Luna immediately turned and ran the other way.

The Daemon laughed, the sound like a thousand fingernails scraping across a chalkboard, and Luna knew it was only toying with her. She ran back to her car and took out her keys, hearing the beast stalk her, feeling the seconds race by like a whirlwind. Her hands were shaking so bad it took her a couple tries to unlock the back door.

She immediately spotted the handle of the fire axe and reached for it.

The Daemon grabbed her arm and wrenched it, pulling her shoulder clean from its socket and she fell hard to the broken ground. When she could breathe past the pain she pulled on her captured arm and reached out with her good one. Her fingers barely touched the end of the axe and she choked back a scream of frustration.

She turned back to the Daemon and kicked out with both her feet, striking it square in the face as it crouched over her like the salivating predator it was. The beast roared, releasing her, rearing back. Luna wasted no time, turning once more and grabbing for the axe, shouting her triumph as she grasped the handle with bone-white fingers and gained her feet, adrenaline aiding her with an almost superhuman speed.

Luna swung the axe violently with her uninjured arm and was rewarded with the beast's tortured scream as the blade sank deep into the side of its head. She jerked on it, pulling it out of the head with a spray of black gore. She immediately swung it again, putting all of her body weight into the blow, and it bit into the creature's hulking shoulder, severing the arm so that it hung lifeless, held only by a string of muscle and tissue.

"*Luna!*" she heard Pulse call out.

The Daemon turned just as Pulse appeared in the lights of the parking lot. Luna swung the axe again, embedding it into the muscles of the beast's back. The Daemon let out a horrible shriek and stumbled to its knees. Luna had to put her foot on its back to wrench the axe free and it shrieked again when she did so, the sound ringing in her ears.

"Stand clear!" Pulse raised his hands and a bolt of silver-blue lightning shot from his fingertips, straight into the Daemon's chest. The smell of burning, rotting flesh was thick in her nostrils now. The beast screamed and jerked violently as the bolt of energy seared through muscle and bone, to the beating heart in its chest.

The beast's chest exploded outward as the heart caught fire within its flesh. Luna ran to Pulse's side and watched as he sent another bolt of lightning straight into the monster. The creature screamed again and Luna put her hands over her ears to block out the horrific sound. It twitched then lay still on the ground where it fell, lifelessly. Pulse sent one more bolt into the Daemon and its carcass caught fire, burning the remains to ash.

"Are you all right?"

She nodded, wincing. "Yeah. But I think my shoulder is out of its socket." She moved her injured arm and winced again.

Pulse immediately laid his hands on her affected shoulder. Warmth radiated out of his palms, straight to the pain of her injury. With a gasp, she felt the bone slip back into place. Strangely, it didn't hurt. It was merely a little uncomfortable, a little alien. The soreness eased and Pulse's warmth filled her, leaving only a memory of the pain behind.

"Thank you," she croaked in a hoarse voice. She turned and walked to her car, looking about her vehicle until she found her bag of supplies, then went back to his side.

"Is that your only injury?" he asked, watching her move stiffly, concerned.

"Yeah." She sighed and leaned against him. "I'm just tired." He put his arm around her, pulling her close. "Let's get out of here."

Pulse tightened his arms around her and the world immediately fell away.

Chapter Eleven

ജ

Luna opened her eyes and gasped with delight.

She was standing in the center of a great, vast room. It was so large she felt dwarfed, tiny. The walls and floor looked as though they had been carved out of rock — gray rock with little twinkles of crystal in it. The ceiling was so high that the dim light of the room didn't touch it, leaving it cast in shades of darkness.

Luna was overwhelmed by her surroundings. Rugs of rich hues littered the stone floor and hung on some of the walls, taking a little of the starkness out of the massive room. It was warm and cozy, inviting. A large, plush crimson couch was in the center of the room, as well as two throne-like chairs of matching color. There were sconces on the walls. They weren't lit by fire, but by a strange ball of warm, bright light.

It smelled like Pulse here, she realized with a contented smile as she breathed the spicy, sexy scent deep into her lungs. She pulled out of Pulse's arms and walked about the room, noting the intricate carvings on the bookshelves that lined one of the walls, studying the large painted portraits of men and women who each looked a little bit like Pulse.

While she looked around, Pulse lit a roaring fire in the fireplace that was twice as tall as she was. It crackled happily, filling the room with more light, more warmth. Luna passed by the fireplace and went into the next room — a bedroom. The room was almost as large as the sitting room, and the ceilings were just as high. In the center of the room there was a huge canopy bed, with elaborate carvings etched into the dark wood. Fantastical creatures and exotic flowers were but a few of the many designs.

Luna went through another door in the bedroom and found the bathroom. Everything within was made of stone—the sunken tub, the large shower stall, the strangely shaped toilet. There was a massive, gold-trimmed mirror on one wall and she caught sight of her reflection. She looked miniscule in the great, open space, and strangely vulnerable. Luna looked away and continued her exploration.

On the other side of the sitting room was a door that led into a small kitchen. There were no modern appliances here, just a strange wood stove and a wooden ice chest filled with perishable goods. It wasn't a large room, but again the ceilings were so high here that she couldn't see them.

When she was done with her exploration, she once more joined Pulse in the sitting room.

"I must now go and inform the Council that we have arrived," he told her. "Would you like to come with me?"

Luna nodded with a smile. Pulse reached out and took her hand in his, and led her to the door. He opened it, gently pushing her out into the passageway, and she gasped.

You could have fit several RVs front to back in the hall, it was that grand. Every few feet there was a lit sconce on the wall, providing dim, warm light to see by. There were doors placed here and there along the way, and Luna wondered what kind of people she might find behind them. Pulse was the only Shikar she'd ever met and she was especially looking forward to seeing what the others looked like.

They walked for a long time. She was beginning to grow winded, having to walk faster to keep up with Pulse's long strides, when they came to a set of stone doors.

Pulse pushed them open, revealing the largest room she'd seen yet. There was a massive round table in the center of the room, with elaborate thrones tucked around it. There was also a fireplace at one end of the enormous room, and Pulse lit it to roaring life. He reached into a bejeweled box on the mantel and pulled out a handful of what looked like sand.

"This is fl'shan powder," he explained. "It has many uses, including communication," he said, turning and throwing the powder into the fire. The flame roared high and white then settled back down. "I call forth those of the Council who would speak with me," he said into the fire, voice booming with authority.

"Take a seat," he told her, motioning towards one of the thrones. "They will be here soon."

Luna sat, but she was beginning to have second thoughts. "Maybe I shouldn't be here," she said warily, suddenly nervous.

"You should," he countered. "You will have a role to play here, one of great importance. You will help to guide us in some of our decision-making. You should meet everyone as soon as possible, if they are to put their trust in you at all."

Luna clasped her hands in her lap and tried not to fidget anxiously. Just when she was beginning to wonder if anyone was coming, the double doors flew open and admitted four men.

Never in her life had she seen such a sight. The men were all well built, heavily muscled and tall. Not one of them stood below six and a half feet. All but one had long, beautiful hair more suitable for a woman than a man. They all looked about the same age as Pulse, none of them showing age beyond thirty or perhaps forty years.

The men looked at her and then looked pointedly at Pulse.

"I will explain everything once the others arrive," he told them softly, firmly.

The men nodded, their faith in Pulse absolute, and took seats around the table. Luna ignored their curious stares and twiddled her thumbs anxiously. Pulse still stood tall and proud by the massive fireplace, waiting.

Seven more men entered, each a beautiful work of art, talking quietly amongst themselves. They fell into silence upon seeing Luna and took their seats without another word, watching her curiously. Again, Luna ignored their stares and focused instead on her lap.

"We are only missing Tryton now," Pulse said. "Thank you all for coming on such short notice. I hadn't expected all of you." The men nodded their responses. They were all so serious, so quiet, Luna felt dwarfed by their presence.

Just then another man walked in with powerful strides. He had long, shining blond hair and dark skin, darker than the others in the room. His eyes, like those of everyone present, were filled with golden fire that nearly glowed. He noticed her with a small start and smiled, a friendly smile. Luna was thankful to him for that.

Pulse stepped away from the fireplace as the newcomer—Tryton—took his seat next to her. All thirteen seats were full now and Luna shifted uncomfortably in the crowd of staring eyes.

"I call this meeting to order," Tryton said aloud in perfect English. "Tell us why you have brought us here, Generator," he said, speaking to Pulse.

Generator? Well, she supposed he was like an electric generator of sorts. It was as apt a title as any.

"As you know, I traveled to the surface—by Grimm, was it only a few days ago?" He looked surprised at the realization.

"Did you find what you sought?" Tryton asked, and his voice resounded in her mind like the ringing of ancient bells.

Pulse snapped back, his customary mask falling back into place. "I did. Friends, I wish to introduce you to my woman, Luna."

The way he called her "my woman" made chills race down her spine. There were a few gasps but no one spoke. Everyone's eyes centered on her and Luna felt her cheeks heat with a blush at all the attention she was getting.

"She single-handedly convinced me that humanity is worth saving." Pulse's warm gaze swept over her and Luna blushed harder.

"I am most pleased to hear this," Tryton said. "Though we all know of humans' penchant for self-destruction, we also know that we have a responsibility as higher beings to protect those weaker than us."

"I see that now." Pulse nodded. "I am glad of it."

"And I am glad for you." Tryton smiled at her and winked. Luna was shocked at the strangely human gesture.

"Luna is a precog," Pulse said softly. "She can predict the future better than any seer I have ever met. However, her visions are those of negative happenings yet to come, not positive ones. I thought, perhaps, she could be of some use to us."

Tryton nodded thoughtfully. "Precognitives are rare and special, even among our own kind. She could be of great use to our Voyeurs." He turned to Luna. "Our spies," he explained for her patiently with a soft, wry chuckle. "As well as a valuable asset to our Council."

"I can't pick and choose my predications," Luna cautioned. "And it may be weeks before I have another. I can't promise you anything."

Tryton smiled. "We shall have to be patient and see what happens."

"I destroyed two Daemons tonight on the surface. They were hunting us both, within the New York City limits," Pulse revealed without warning.

Tryton sat back, his face going cold and serious. "They grow too bold," he said with a growl.

"My sentiments exactly," Pulse agreed. "Anyone could have seen them, and our battle. I do not think there were any witnesses, but there is no way to be certain."

"We shall have to send the Voyeurs into the Territories to investigate and ensure that there were no witnesses," one of the men said, a tall, lithe man with bright blond hair.

The others seconded the motion immediately. "I agree," Tryton murmured. "If there were any witnesses we must know who they are and where they call home. We will have to erase some memories, but that is par for the course. I am curious, though. Why did they take such a risk?"

"I think it is because Luna has eluded them for so long, and once they had their chance to attack they took it without thought to the possible consequences," Pulse explained.

"Daemons used to fear public places above all else. They feared death at the hands of frightened civilians—and with good reason." Tryton shook his head. "It seems that a great many things have changed in recent years."

"Where do they keep coming from? We defeated so many at the Gates that it is a wonder any of them survived. Yet still they bedevil us, growing stronger with each passing day," one of the men said.

Tryton pursed his full lips. "They are making more and more of the beasts themselves. No longer do they rely on the Lord of the Horde for strength. They prey on innocents, consuming all the raw power their victims have to give. They cling to survival with a surprising strength. I think, before long, that they will make a grave error and alert the citizens of the Territories to their presence."

"We must get the Voyeurs out there as soon as possible, to contain such a serious threat," a man with long, ebony hair said.

"I agree with this as well." Tryton sighed heavily and turned to Pulse. "Call the Voyeurs forth, Generator."

Pulse retrieved another fistful of the fl'shan powder and threw it into the fire. "Come, Voyeurs, we have need of you," he said into the roaring flame.

Tryton turned to look at Luna with his all too knowing golden eyes. "So your visions are of negative things. Have you ever tried to change the course of your predictions?" he asked curiously.

Luna nodded. "Nearly every time I have one. But until the other night, when Pulse helped me, I had never been able to succeed in changing things."

"Fate is hard to change," Tryton agreed, and Luna could see in his eyes that he really understood her plight. "It takes great strength and will to alter the course of events already set in motion. I would think it nearly impossible to change the future, once it has been written. You are brave to try."

Luna shrugged. "I'm not brave. I'm just stubborn." She grinned at him, feeling her heart soften towards him though they had only just barely met.

Tryton and some of the others laughed.

The double doors opened inward and thirteen women and one man came into the room. The man, Luna noted with shock, was a human—or at least his eyes were different from any of the Shikars around him. He held hands with one of the women, a beautiful, curvaceous girl who eyed Luna with great interest.

"Come forward," Tryton told them.

Luna was amazed at how beautiful each woman was in her own special, unique way. She was struck dumb by their natural grace and beauty, which they exhibited so casually. They were lovely, curvaceous and entirely female. She'd never seen anyone like them.

Tryton addressed the group. "There has been a disturbance in the Territories. You will go to New York City and ensure that no one has seen or been attacked by our enemies. If there are witnesses, alter their memories. If there are victims, note each one carefully and make certain that nothing about their deaths will lead back to the Daemons or to us."

"It shall be done, Elder," one of the women said softly. As one, the group turned and swiftly exited the room once more. Luna watched them go curiously. The meeting had taken all of one minute.

Tryton turned back to the Council and to Luna. "When you have a vision, tell us straight away, especially if it concerns one of us or the Daemons. We will decide how to act on your predictions as a group."

One of the Council members nodded. "I am most anxious to hear what she sees."

"I can't promise that I'll come up with anything useful to you or your people," she cautioned once more. "But I will tell you all that I know."

"That is all we can ask," Tryton said solemnly. He looked at Pulse, who was watching Luna's every move with a hungry gaze that no one could have mistaken. "Shall we adjourn this meeting?" Tryton asked with a sly, knowing grin.

Pulse nodded, tearing his eyes away from the woman who so fascinated him. "Luna will stay with me, and we will alert the Council as soon as she has a precognition. Thank you all for coming."

Each of the men gave her a little bow before leaving the room.

Tryton approached Pulse and laid a hand on his shoulder. "Will you change her?" he asked softly.

Luna heard his words and wondered what they meant.

Pulse nodded. "In time," he responded, locking gazes with Luna, freezing all thought in her mind as lust began to overtake her.

Tryton turned to her, startling her out of her trancelike state. "Thank you for convincing Pulse that our cause is just and true." He took her hand and kissed it gallantly. "We owe you a debt we can never repay."

Luna blushed. She couldn't help it. Tryton saw too much, knew too much. She felt naked under his gaze — soul laid bare, secrets uncovered, with no place for her to hide.

Tryton left without another word, leaving them alone together in the lingering silence of the enormous room. Once the doors had closed behind Tryton, Pulse immediately came to her, eyes hot and full of desire, and bent to capture her mouth with his. Luna couldn't look away from his gaze, and her heart beat a wild staccato in her breast as excitement flooded through her.

A mild, electric shock hit her as their lips touched. Every hair on her body stood on end and her skin broke out in goose bumps. She shivered as he put his arms around her, clutching her close. Her nipples hardened as he pressed her tight to his chest, making her catch her breath.

His tongue entered her mouth like a dream. It was hot and sweet and smooth, like wet silk between her lips. She sucked on his tongue, reveling in the groan that tore free from his throat, swallowing the sound and returning it with one of her own.

Pulse backed her up to the table then lifted her onto it with one arm around her waist. Luna gasped as he sucked her tongue into his mouth, fingers digging into the flesh of her hips. He licked her lips erotically, before once more plunging his tongue in to taste and tease.

His hands tore at her shirt, ripping it from throat to stomach. Her breasts were bared to his gaze and to his touch. He took hold of her nipple between his thumb and forefinger and squeezed it until it was long and thick and hard, then his fingers moved to the other one, playing with her sensitive skin until she was gasping for breath.

Pulse palmed her breasts, squeezing them, testing their weight. She arched into him, skin so sensitive that his lightest touch made her entire body hum. His clever hands skimmed over her belly and settled on the fastening of her jeans.

He undid the button and slowly, teasingly pulled down the zipper. The sound of the sliding zipper enflamed their senses. It echoed in the silence of the room like a thunderclap.

When he had her jeans opened he removed her shoes, tracing his fingers down the soles of her feet. Then he lifted her with one powerful hand and removed her jeans with the other, tugging them off her feet and tossing them to the floor.

Pulse pushed her back so that she lay on the table with her legs dangling off the edge. He pulled her panties off and stared rapt at what he had uncovered. His eyes burned her where they roved over her nudity, taking in the sight of her bare, aching breasts with the thickly rouged nipples stabbing towards the heavens, her pink, glistening pussy fully open to his gaze like the bloom of a flower.

He reached out with one finger and traced it down the seam of her labia. Then he spread her pussy lips apart with his fingers and looked at the treasure he had uncovered. He growled a low, hungry sound and bent, spreading her legs wider with his shoulders.

Luna felt the cool air on her most sensitive places and shivered deliciously. Pulse bent his head and licked her, spearing his tongue inside her, filling her, making her ache with need. She couldn't close her legs if she wanted to — which she didn't — not with Pulse's broad shoulders wedged between them. She had no secrets from him, no veil to hide behind. She was laid utterly bare before him.

He splayed his hands wide and ran them down her chest, breasts, belly and lower. He stroked her like he would a cat, over and over, and she arched into his touch as if she was one. But her skin sang with a craving for a deeper touch, and she moaned brokenly as he continued to tease and torment her.

She wanted his cock. And she wanted it now.

Fisting her hands in his hair, she tugged mercilessly but Pulse ignored her struggles and continued to control the situation. He blew gently on her exposed, wet flesh and she cried out. He touched her with one finger, pressing into the swollen ache of her clit, and licked her thoroughly, causing her to thrash uncontrollably beneath his ministrations.

His tongue filled her with liquid fire. He thrust it to the depths of her, stretching her, tasting all she had to give. Luna cried out and bucked underneath him.

"Please, Pulse. *Please*," she begged.

He came up over her body, covering hers with his. His eyes were fierce as flames as he locked gazes with her. "Tell me what you want," he commanded.

"I want *you*," she gasped, wrapping her legs around his waist, trying to seat herself against his erection. He held her hips back with his hands, keeping her from her goal. She yelled wordlessly in mounting frustration.

"Tell me exactly what you want," he commanded once more, patiently.

Luna shivered delicately. "I want you to fuck me," she said breathlessly. "I want you to fuck my pussy until I scream."

His fingers thrust into her, making her gasp. "You want me to fuck this pussy?" he asked.

"Yes, *yes*," she gasped.

"Tell me your pussy is mine and mine alone, and I might oblige you…if I'm ready," he teased, releasing his cock with one hand as he watched her.

Luna shrieked, disgruntled to the point of madness. "My pussy is yours," she moaned. "It's yours, it's yours, *it's yours*!"

"Shall I fuck my pussy now?" he asked devilishly.

"*Yes!*" she screamed.

From one heartbeat to the next, they had left the table and were lying on Pulse's bed. He had Traveled them there even as the echo of her shout died away in their ears.

Pulse thrust into her so hard it took her breath away. He filled her to overflowing, stretching her tight around his hard, pulsing girth. When she had the breath to scream, the sound came brokenly through her love-swollen lips and she strained beneath his possession, writhing uncontrollably. Rolling her hips until he was seated to the hilt deep within her.

The thick, plum-shaped crown of him pressed into a magical spot inside her. He thrust and withdrew, rubbing his cock on that spot until she saw stars behind her eyes.

It felt as if a fist was hammering at her, but the sensation was so delicious it made tears stream from the corners of her eyes. He stretched her to the breaking point, filling her deeply, consuming her body and soul. All she could do was hold on during the storm, riding him as he was riding her, rolling her hips to take him even deeper.

The wet sounds their bodies made together heightened their senses, a sensual song with a rhythm as old as time searing itself into their brains. A lone droplet of sweat fell from his forehead onto her mouth and she licked the salty tear away with her tongue, causing Pulse to growl hungrily, eyes glued to her lips.

He was thrusting so hard into her that she moved bodily up and down on the mattress, her hair a tangle about her face, her skin warm from the friction at her front and back. His expert fingers moved between their bodies to toy with her clit. Luna cried out and bucked uncontrollably beneath him, wanting more of the delightful sensations his fingers visited upon her.

On a downward thrust, he put a finger inside her alongside his cock. This stretched her flesh so tightly that she was breathless. He hooked the finger and found that magical spot within that was sure to undo her.

And it did.

With a scream, Luna clutched him to her and came so violently that her body shook with the tremors. Her pussy milked his cock with tiny pulsations and he groaned, reveling in the tightness of her sheath. His thumb stroked her clit while his finger thrust in and out of her and her climax pushed them both up into the heavens.

Pulse came with a roar, jerking free of her body, spending himself on the sheets. He covered her mouth with his and kissed her until her brain was a mush of jumbled thoughts and emotions. She clutched him to her as she rode the storm, finally shuddering one last time before going still.

Pulse lay down next to her, careful to keep their bodies touching. He spooned her, pulling her hair out of her face and tucking it behind her ear. He kissed the shell of her ear and settled in behind her.

The sweat cooled on their bodies and they both fell into a deep, well-deserved slumber.

Chapter Twelve
Four days later

ॐ

Luna awoke to the feel of Pulse's lips on her pussy.

For four days they had stayed in bed, getting up only to bathe and call for food to be brought in by one of the kitchen women. Luna's body was bruised and sore from all the loving, but she reveled in each pull of her muscles, each tiny pain a reminder of his fierce possession. She bore his love marks on her breasts, belly and even the tender flesh of her inner thighs. He had marked her as his.

She had made her claim on him as well. His throat and shoulders were red with hickeys, his back pink from the raking of her nails each time she came. He was hers, just as surely as she was his.

One thing bothered her, though. Pulse never spent himself inside her body. Nor did he let her suck him until he came in her mouth. He was careful not to let any of his seed enter her. She wondered why, knowing there was likely a good reason that he held himself back. She just wished she knew what that reason was so she could better understand what went on inside his mind.

Now Pulse speared her with his tongue, so hot it burned her tender skin. She cried out and arched up into his touch, wanting a deeper claiming. He rained kisses down upon her wet flesh until she was mindless with hunger.

Now he came up her body, kissing every inch of skin that he passed, until he was lying atop her. Her breasts were pressed against his chest, making her nipples ache, stealing away her breath. He claimed her mouth, filling it with his tongue that still tasted of her.

He pulled away and grabbed something from the bedside table. Luna watched raptly as he opened a foil packet and began to roll a condom over his thick, purple length. Then his hands came back to her and spread her legs wide. He entered her with one fierce thrust, seating himself to the hilt so that his sac slapped against her bottom. Luna cried out and arched beneath him, rolling her hips to accept him deeper within her aching, soaking-wet pussy. He began a primitive rhythm, thrust and withdrawal, guiding her to follow him. They moved together like a dream, like liquid desire, gazes locked and hearts entwined.

Luna heard the laughter and the knock on the door one split second before two Council members came into the room. Both were tall and well built, beautiful to look at. Beautiful but wholly masculine. One had long, shining blond hair while the other had wavy, jet-black hair, but they were both striking in their coloring and their eyes fairly glowed. The men fell silent as they saw Pulse and Luna tangled together on the bed.

"Sabre, Lance, what do you two want?" Pulse growled, never once slowing his pace, thrusting into her, uncaring that they had an audience.

Luna felt her face heat in a brilliant blush. She tried to push Pulse away, but he would not release her. She tried to pull the covers up over them, but Pulse pushed them back down, pulling her legs around his waist so that he could thrust even harder, even deeper into her.

The men watched them, desire hot and bright in both their gazes. "We have come regarding the grain harvest," the blond-haired man said.

"How goes it, Sabre?" Pulse thrust in and out of her until she was mindless to their audience—or almost. It felt so good she didn't care that others saw, and that brought another blush to her cheeks.

Both men were looking at the wet, pink flesh of her pussy as it swallowed Pulse's cock over and over. "It goes well. We will have a large surplus this season," Sabre said raggedly.

Pulse gave her a wicked look that melted her insides. "Come closer," he said to the two men.

Sabre and Lance immediately came to the bed, one on each side. Pulse shoved into her hard and she cried out, head thrashing on the pillow, painfully aware of the two men who stood but an arm's length away but so caught up in her passion that she couldn't care.

"May we touch her?" Lance whispered, staring raptly down at her nude, glistening body.

Pulse's gaze was hot on hers. "What say you, love?" he asked.

Luna was beyond speech. Never in her life did she think she'd find herself in this position, and now that she did, she decided it would be fun to experiment. Maybe. If she didn't die of embarrassment first.

She didn't have to say anything. The two men saw the acceptance, the excitement in her gaze and knew what she wanted. Sabre crawled towards her and popped one of Luna's nipples into his mouth, sucking on it so that she saw stars. Lance pinched her other nipple with his thumb and forefinger, rolling it until it was hard as a diamond and darkly rouged like a berry.

Luna cried out uncontrollably and bucked beneath Pulse. Sabre bit delicately into her flesh with his teeth, wringing a gasp from her dry lips. Lance came down and slurped her other nipple into his mouth, tonguing it until it ached deliciously. Her body trembled as it was bombarded by exquisite sensations.

As the two men sucked on her nipples, Pulse increased the pace and strength of his thrusts. Luna felt sure she would bruise but she didn't care. She welcomed the ache, the pleasure-pain of his possession, and craved even more. Tangling her fingers in Sabre's and Lance's hair, she clutched them closer to her, arching into their wet, hot mouths with a low moan.

Pulse's fingers moved between them, finding her clit. He rubbed the tiny nubbin of flesh, making her wetter, making her clench his cock tighter inside her cunt with tiny, fluttering vibrations. The tips of his fingers shocked her, but lightly, as he pressed little circles into her clit, using her own wetness to ease his motions.

Luna's vision grayed out. The two wet, hot mouths sucking on her nipples made her dizzy with desire. The feel of Pulse's cock impaling her over and over, stretching her nearly to the point of pain, made her entire body shake with delicate tremors. It was too much sensation all at once, bombarding her with pleasure until tears again sprang from the corners of her eyes.

She came with a scream. The climax was so sudden and so intense that she went stiff beneath the three men, straining upwards with a cry. Her pussy throbbed, milking Pulse's cock with pulsating convulsions. Her entire body felt swollen, ravaged and entirely loved.

Pulse shoved Lance and Sabre off her with none too gentle motions. The two men fell back, breath rasping in their lungs. Luna felt Pulse surge into her one last time and he came with a roar, shooting his semen into the tip of the condom, burning her insides.

Pulse collapsed on top of her. Lance and Sabre rose and looked down at the two lovers with lust-filled gazes.

Suddenly, Luna's eyes flared open. She reached out and grabbed Sabre's hand with hers. "You have to come with us," she said.

"What?" he asked with a puzzled frown.

Luna swallowed hard. "There will be an attack. In Tennessee. Tonight. A girl and her parents will be in danger—the Daemons will eat them if they get the chance. There will be many monsters—nine, I think—and you must come with us when Pulse and I try to fight them off."

Pulse pulled back, the shock of his cock leaving her body making her gasp. "*We're* not going," he told her, pulling off his condom and laying it on the bedside table. "I shall send some of my warriors to aid this family, but we will stay here. Where you are safe."

Luna shook her head. "No. We have to go. And Sabre has to be there, too. Don't ask me why—I don't know—but we can't send anyone in our place. I've never had a premonition like this, so I don't understand it. But I know we have to go ourselves. It's important."

Sabre nodded solemnly. "I am ever at your side, Generator," he said formally.

Pulse glared at him and the two men turned and left the room. Now Pulse looked back at Luna, and she saw the worry and the frustration in his eyes. "Don't worry," she said. "It's not too cold in Tennessee this time of year. I won't die." She tried to smile, but couldn't quite manage it. She let out a heartfelt sigh and gazed at Pulse. He still looked so worried. It hurt her heart to know that she was the reason for it. She lay on her side, putting her hands beneath her head and meeting Pulse's superheated gaze.

"I love you," she said quietly, before she could even think to call the words back.

Pulse's eyes went wide. "Say that again," he commanded.

Luna was afraid, but she swallowed her fear and took the plunge. "I love you," she said once more, louder.

He grabbed her to him and rolled until she was seated atop him. He reached for her breasts, gently flicking the nipples with his thumbs. "Say it again."

"I love you!" she laughed, helpless to stem the joy that filled her heart.

"I shall never tire of hearing the words," he said, closing his eyes to savor the moment. "You must tell me and tell me often."

"I will." She shivered beneath his clever hands as he continued to toy with her nipples, making them swell and ache for the erotic possession of his mouth.

Pulse eased her off him before sitting up and getting out of bed. He walked to the large, ornately carved wooden armoire in one corner of the room and began rooting around in it for clothing.

"It is almost night in Tennessee now. If we are going to go, you must hurry and dress," he warned her.

"How do you know it's almost night?" she asked.

"I can sense it," he told her simply.

"But that doesn't give me any time to plan," she wailed, punching the pillows in frustration.

He looked at her, fiery gaze drinking in the sight of her nudity like a man dying of thirst. "You don't need to plan anything. Sabre and I will fight off the Daemons, while you protect the family. It's really quite simple."

"No, it's not," she protested. "I've never had a premonition with so little notice! I usually have plenty of time to prepare, to go over what I must do in my mind. I don't like this."

"Do you know what time they will strike?" he asked, diverting her attention a little.

Luna thought for a moment. "I think around midnight. The witching hour. I think the Daemons favor that time for some reason."

"It is true, they are at their peak in the dead of night," he agreed. "It will make our job more difficult, but it will not be an insurmountable hurdle. Sabre and I can easily handle the Daemons. While *you*," he pinned her with his gaze, "take care to stay out of the way of danger."

Luna harrumphed. "I'm not the one in danger here, remember? I won't die."

"But you might get hurt," he said stonily.

Luna had to agree with that—she had no way of knowing if she would be hurt or not, only that it wouldn't be a mortal wound. "Okay. I'll stay out of your way while you take care of the Daemons," she conceded.

"Good," he grunted, putting on a pair of loose black trousers and a matching black tunic, both articles of clothing made from a soft, alien-looking material.

Luna got up and went to find her duffel bag of possessions. She found it in the sitting room, tossed negligently on one of the throne-like chairs. She immediately dug into it and found some clothing, dressing hurriedly in jeans, a T-shirt and tennis shoes. She put her hair up with an elastic band, pulling the ponytail tight against her head, and went back into the bedroom to join Pulse.

"I will take a short meeting with Tryton, to let him know our destination and purpose," Pulse said. "He will want to be kept abreast of the situation."

"Can I come with you?" she asked.

Pulse nodded, lacing up heavy black boots with silver buckles on them. "I think Tryton will want to see you as well, to hear your prediction from your own lips."

"Cool."

"Come. We don't have much time to waste." He took her hand and led her out of the room, which she hadn't left once in almost five days.

The first door he stopped at was answered by Sabre, who, it seemed, had been waiting on them. He came out of his apartment, shutting the door firmly behind him. The three of them proceeded onward to Tryton's personal quarters.

When Pulse knocked on the door they heard Tryton's call for them to enter. Luna stayed behind Pulse, her hand still held captive in his. She peeked around him and saw that Tryton already had company. A man and a woman watched her curiously as they entered the sitting room, and Luna felt her cheeks blush under their close regard.

Tryton rose from his seat and greeted them. "Luna, I would like you to meet my two most formidable warriors, Cady and Obsidian."

Luna nodded to each of them in turn, but she couldn't help but wonder. "I didn't know there were any women warriors," she said.

Cady grinned and Luna liked her immediately. There was something so spirited and free about the small woman that she couldn't help but respond to Cady with a smile of her own. "Actually, there aren't many. And I was the first," Cady told her proudly. "Sid here still has a hard time accepting it, but I am a warrior and a warrior I will stay, no matter how much he protests."

"Are you and Obsidian—" She stopped, thinking carefully on her words.

Cady nodded her head as if she knew what Luna was asking. And she did. "Obsidian and I are mated. Though it seems I lament that truth daily." She cast a devilish glance at her husband, who merely snorted arrogantly.

"What has brought you to my chambers?" Tryton asked them curiously.

"Luna has had a premonition," Pulse said.

Tryton looked at her and Luna blushed under his intense gaze. "Tell me your prediction," he commanded gently.

Luna took a deep breath. "Tonight there will be a large attack by the Daemons. There will be a lot of them. They will kill a small family in rural Tennessee and take the daughter as a hostage. I don't know why," she apologized. "But I *do* know where they live—it's a small soybean farm in Greeneville, in northeast Tennessee."

"Good," Tryton said. "That will save us much time searching. But why must you and Pulse and—I assume, since you're here, Sabre, that you're going too? Why not send some warriors in to get the job done? This task is beneath a Council member, let alone two."

"I have to go and make sure no one gets hurt," Luna explained. "And Sabre absolutely has to be there—don't ask me why."

Tryton nodded. "Can you tell me the outcome of this altercation?" he asked.

Luna shook her head. "All I know is that if we don't go the parents will die and they'll have a powerful hostage. The girl, she's telekinetic," she said, the knowledge coming to her suddenly. "The Daemons don't want her dead, they want her alive."

Understanding dawned in Tryton's eyes. "You are certain?"

"Yes," she said with a heavy sigh. "And I'm afraid that if Pulse doesn't come I won't be able to change the outcome of my premonition. It seems he's the only one who can help me actually make a difference."

Tryton studied the three of them for a long moment. "Very well then. I shall trust that you know what you are doing." He smiled. "Just be sure you bring yourselves back unharmed."

"Wait," she said. "I need some kind of a weapon. No way am I going in there empty-handed."

Cady bounded to her feet and swiftly, efficiently pulled a Glock 9mm from a leg holster. She handed it to Luna, who looked down at the weapon with a lump of fear in her throat. "I've never fired a gun before," she admitted, hefting the weight of the weapon in her hand.

"All you do is point this end away from you and pull the trigger. I've already taken the safety off. Just aim and shoot and stay as far away from the Daemons as you can."

"Thank you," Luna murmured and tucked the gun into the waist of her jeans in the small of her back, carefully though, as she might have handled a viper.

Cady only grinned mischievously before once more joining her husband.

"It is already dark in Tennessee," Tryton said.

"We must leave at once," Pulse told them.

Both Sabre and Pulse bowed respectfully to Tryton and the two warriors. Tugging on her hand, Pulse turned and led the way out of Tryton's room. Once out in the passageway, he turned to her and smiled tenderly.

"Picture your destination in your mind. Think hard on where we must go," he instructed softly.

Luna nodded and fixed her thoughts on the image of the large soybean farm, with its many acres situated out in the middle of nowhere. She focused on the image of the family, the eighteen-year-old daughter especially, and took a deep, calming breath. "Okay," she said.

"I will Travel, but you will lead us there," Pulse said. "Just keep the image of our destination strong in your mind."

They joined hands, Luna, Pulse and Sabre, and the world fell away beneath their feet, stealing her breath away.

Chapter Thirteen

ഗ

It was pitch-black when they arrived on the outskirts of the farm. Luna looked around—you could see for half a mile at least in every direction and most of that ground was covered in soybean plants. In the very center of the several acre spread was a modest house, the many windows alight from within. There was no one about.

Luna felt exposed. She didn't want to be out in the open like this—a moving target for their enemies—but there were no trees behind which to hide. Only the darkness shrouded them, obscuring them from any curious eyes.

They approached the house on quiet feet, making hardly a sound as they found their way through the maze of plants. Pulse led the way, followed closely by Luna and Sabre.

All was silent save the loud cacophony of chirping crickets and the calls of cicadas. A bird cried out in the darkness and Pulse immediately ducked down close to the ground. Luna and Sabre quickly joined him, squatting low behind him, looking around for any possible threat. Several minutes passed. The sound did not come again and they all relaxed, continuing on their way.

A low, cool fog spread out over the ground, obscuring their vision a little. It gave the land an eerie, ominous feel, and Luna didn't like it one bit. The smell of the earth was strong here, as if it had just recently been tilled. Luna felt a great weight pressing down on her and she knew that she must try her best to focus on that apprehension, for any warning she could give the two men would be useful.

"They will appear right here," she said, freezing in place. "Most of them, anyway. The others..." She thought for a moment. "The others will spread out and attack the house directly while you're busy taking care of these Daemons."

"They are using decoys," Sabre growled. "To draw us away from their main target."

"I will see to the Daemons here," Pulse told her. "Sabre, you can concentrate on keeping the bastards away from the house. Luna, you will watch over the family and alert me if there is the threat of any immediate danger. Understood?"

Both Luna and Sabre nodded solemnly.

They hunched down there, still a ways from the house, and waited. Luna glanced at her watch and gasped. It was only ten minutes to midnight. They had precious little time left.

"Ten minutes, guys," she warned. "I'm going to go to the house and meet the family."

Pulse grabbed her wrist as she rose. "Be cautious. We are all in much danger here."

"Okay."

He didn't let go of her. "I don't like this. Perhaps you should go back home—"

"No," she said firmly. "I have to be sure they're all right. I have to see for myself."

Pulse sighed heavily and Sabre watched them curiously. "I know you do," he said. "But I still don't like it."

"Yeah, well, that's life." She shrugged with a carelessness she didn't feel. "I'll be all right. I know how I die—and it's not here. Not tonight. Everything will be okay."

Sabre started and looked at her, hard. "You know how you're going to die?"

Luna nodded. "I'm going to freeze to death."

"Do you know when?" he asked, quite obviously shocked to his toes.

"No," she replied nonchalantly, too focused on what was to come to really pay much attention to the conversation.

"Doesn't this knowledge drive you mad?" Sabre's eyes were wide with incredulity.

"No," she said with forced patience, carefully observing their shadowy surroundings. "In fact, I think it's helpful to know how I'll die. I don't have to be afraid of situations like this, for example—I know I won't be mortally wounded or anything like that."

"It also makes her careless," Pulse said quietly, drawing her full attention at last. "Do not put yourself in danger tonight simply because you know you won't die. You may not die, but you *may* be hurt very badly. You must stay out of the path of danger and let Sabre and me do our duty. I don't want to have to worry about you."

Luna kissed him, uncaring that Sabre watched them carefully. "I'll be fine," she told him. "Now I have to go and introduce myself to the family before the monsters get here." She trudged off in the direction of the house.

Pulse watched her go with a pang in his heart. Then he turned his attention back to the task at hand. Luna was on her own now. He had to trust that she knew what she was doing.

* * * * *

A short, dumpy woman with graying hair answered the door after Luna's knock. She smiled, but there was a puzzled look in her eyes, probably owing to the late hour. "Yes?"

Luna took a deep breath. "My name is Luna. I've come to tell you something that may shock you."

A man joined the woman at the door. He was much taller than she, with a barrel chest and white hair. "What's going on?" he asked by way of greeting.

"This woman says she has something to tell us," the woman explained.

"May I come in?" Luna asked gently.

The woman eyed her suspiciously for a moment then nodded her acquiescence. "Come on in. I was just putting away a casserole I made for tomorrow's dinner—have you eaten?"

"I'm fine, thank you." Luna crossed the threshold and looked at the cozy surroundings of the old house. The man, still at the woman's side, watched her closely.

"What are your names?" Luna asked softly.

"I'm Lillith, and this is my husband Elijah. My daughter, Apple, is in the living room watching TV. Though it's so late she really should be in bed—she has a big test tomorrow. Come on in and have a seat."

Luna followed them into the living room. She saw the girl sitting on the floor in front of a large-screen TV. Her hair was black with blue tips, cut short so that she could wear it in spikes all around her head. She had a labret piercing, just below her pouting lower lip, the jewelry twinkling in the light. Her eyes were the darkest, purest green Luna had ever seen and those eyes bore into her with wisdom far beyond the girl's years. Apple was quietly studying her, but she didn't look at all alarmed.

Nor did she look like someone who could bring about the end of the world. But Luna knew better.

The girl turned back to the television, dismissing her, and Luna was glad to be out from under her piercing gaze. Lillith motioned for her to sit on the couch and she did so, glancing at her watch nervously.

She plunged in, knowing there was precious little time. "I'm sorry to disturb you so late, but I've come to warn you of something terrible that's about to happen."

Elijah groaned and sat heavily in a well-worn armchair. Luna ignored him and continued on, speaking to Lillith. "There's going to be an attack here tonight. You and your family are in serious danger. You have to arm yourselves and prepare for a fight."

"Look, lady, if this is some kind of prank—" Elijah started.

Luna interrupted him. "This is no prank, I'm sorry to say. And I am *very* serious when I say that your lives are in danger. Especially your daughter's. This isn't a joke or a scam. I just want to help you. I swear it." She glanced down at her watch again and blanched. Time was flying by far too swiftly. Any minute now the attack would begin. She had to get these people moving. Now.

Apple turned away from the TV and eyed Luna curiously. "Who wants to hurt us?"

"This is going to sound crazy, I know. But there are monsters after you. They're coming here any minute and they only want one thing—to destroy your lives," Luna explained hurriedly.

Elijah rose from his chair angrily. "That's enough nonsense. Please leave *now*."

Apple rose from the floor and went to one of the large windows. She peered out, putting her hand up over her eyes to block out the light. "I don't see any—"

The front door opened with a tremendous crash. Luna flew to her feet and looked around. "Where's the back door?" she shouted.

Lillith was the first to come out of her shocked surprise. "Follow me," she said, eyes dawning in realization of the danger mounting around her.

But it was too late. A seven-foot-tall Daemon bounded into the room with a vicious growl. It swung its massive, spike-riddled arm and flung the coffee table into the air. It fell to the floor with a crash, splinters of wood flying in every conceivable direction.

Luna pulled the gun from behind her and shot the monster point-blank in the face. Black blood and gore flew out the back of its head as the bullet exploded on exit. The Daemon screamed and the sound struck terror into all their hearts. It charged Luna, taking her down to the floor.

Luna kicked out, unseating the beast. She leveled the gun at it again, this time aiming for the chest, and fired. Blood and tissue sprayed, covering her, hot and sticky and oozing. She rose to her knees and punched her fist into the Daemon's damaged chest.

Her fist sank deep into tissue and sinew. She opened her hand and moved it around inside, seeking out the beating heart. The Daemon reared back, dragging her with it so that she toppled over on top of it. Digging furiously now, Luna held on as the monster struggled to get free.

She felt the slippery heart and sank her fingers into it, nails cutting deep into the muscle. With a violent jerk, she pulled the heart free. It beat a wild tattoo in her hand and she backed away quickly, holding the heart high in triumph.

The Daemon was not yet dead, however. It would not die until the heart was destroyed. It lunged at Luna, taking her once more to the floor. The heart flew from her hands and rolled across the hardwood floor, staining it black. Luna grasped for the organ, only to have it slip, eel-like, through her fingers.

Apple, frozen with shock until now, ran to a glass vase on a high shelf in the room. She threw it to the ground with a resounding crash, glass flying everywhere. She picked up a large, jagged piece of glass and ran to the heart. Apple plunged the glass into the heart, stilling it forever.

The Daemon went limp on Luna, pinning her to the floor painfully with its great weight. She pushed the body off with some difficulty and approached Apple, who was panting heavily, eyes wild with fear. "We have to burn it," she said, motioning towards the heart. "Destroy it completely or it'll get back up again."

Apple grabbed a lighter from atop the television, near an antique oil lamp and set about lighting the heart aflame. Luna grabbed Lillith, who stood frozen with fear and shock. She shook the older woman roughly. "You need to arm yourselves."

The sounds of battle outside the house escalated. Luna heard the growls and screams of several Daemons and shuddered. "Hurry," she told Lillith. The older woman snapped out of her trance and left the room on swift feet.

Elijah gasped for air. "What the hell is that thing?" he rasped.

"That's a Daemon. A monster. They eat humans," Luna explained in a rush of words. "There will be more of them if we don't move. *Now*!"

Apple stamped out the flames that had eaten the heart into ash. There was a large scorch mark in the wood of the floor and the smell of burnt, rotting flesh was thick in the air. "Grab your rifle, Dad," the girl said, and despite the obvious severity of the situation she sounded calm, collected. "Let's get out of here."

Lillith came into the room with the rifle already in her hand. "This is all I could think to find," she apologized.

Luna smiled, or tried to. "It's okay. We just need to get out of these tight quarters — we don't want another Daemon in here this close to us."

Lightning lit the sky, the electromagnetic pulse rattling the windows savagely. Lillith jumped and Apple once more moved to the window and looked out. "Holy crap, there are two gigantic men fighting a bunch of those nasty monster things out there!" the girl exclaimed.

"It's all right," Luna said. "Those men are here to protect you."

"Wow. That blond guy is hot," Apple observed.

Apple kept looking out the window until her mother grabbed her hand, pulling her away. "Come on," she said and led the way out through the back door in the kitchen.

Luna raced outside to the back porch and looked around alertly for any sign of their enemies. Out of the corner of her eye she saw a dark figure emerge mere seconds before it was upon them.

The monster grabbed for Apple first. Luna lunged at it and knocked it backward. It released Apple, who then ran behind her father with a ragged shriek. Luna fired the gun into the beast once, twice, three times, ravaging its chest cavity with bullets. As the beast collapsed back onto the ground she stood over it and plunged her hands in the gore elbows deep and desperately sought out the creature's heart, crushing it with vicious pleasure.

A mist of rain began, and the low-lying fog grew until it was all around them. Luna led the family away from the house, keeping a close watch out for any threat. They made their way several yards into the soybean field when two more Daemons appeared, as if by magic, directly in their path. Luna immediately fired upon them and they disappeared once more.

They reappeared behind them, grabbing once more for Apple. Apple struggled and yelled, beating at the hand of the beast that held her.

A sound like that of a runaway freight train vibrated along the land. Apple shrieked once more and tore free from the monster's grasp. The two beasts advanced upon them. Luna was afraid her premonition—that of the parents' impending deaths—was about to come true.

Without any warning beyond a mounting, roaring cacophony, a large, several-ton rock fell from the heavens and crushed one of the Daemons. Then another and another fell from the sky, striking the ground all around them, making the earth shudder. The rocks were more like enormous boulders and where they came from, Luna couldn't say. They continued to drop, the sky raining stone and water at once.

The remaining Daemon snarled and turned to flee. Luna fired but it ran, making her target difficult. Luna began to chase after it then thought better of it. She needed to stay with this family, to protect them, to make sure they weren't harmed.

Three monsters came running around the house. Apple was the first to spot them, shouting a warning to everyone else. Pulse came around the house, hot on the monsters' trail. He saw Luna and her charges standing among the mighty boulders that had come from the sky. "Get under the porch," he commanded. "Now!"

Luna changed direction and now led the family back under the roof of the back porch. They found shelter in the nick of time. Pulse raised his hand and called the lightning down...but he didn't stop there. Electric charges danced in the water droplets that were raining down still, lighting up the night like a million fireflies. The water struck the Daemons, electrocuting them where they stood, frying them to a crisp.

"Are you all right?" Pulse asked anxiously, rushing to her side as the rain turned once more into a harmless mist, the night going dark around them once more.

Luna could only nod. She couldn't find her voice. She'd never been so happy to see anyone in her life.

Sabre came around the side of the house. "I think that's the lot of them." His eyes roved over the boulders and the family, settling with sudden, searing intensity on Apple, who stared back at him with just as much interest. The two approached each other, Apple stepping off the porch into the rain, uncaring.

When she was but a few feet away from Sabre, Apple paused and regarded him intently. Sabre, looking like he'd been hypnotized by the girl, reached out and slowly traced a gentle line down the girl's cheek with his finger. Apple reached out, put her hand on Sabre's heart and the two stood there, joined, oblivious to the outside world.

Pulse walked around the house a couple times. He burned the carcass of the Daemon Luna had felled and when he was satisfied there were no more monsters about, he joined her and watched the strange byplay between Sabre and Apple.

"We have to erase their memories of this night," Pulse said quietly.

But not quietly enough to keep Elijah from hearing his words. "What are you talking about?" he asked sharply.

Pulse sighed heavily. "Sabre," he called out. "It's time."

Sabre tore his gaze away from Apple's and met Pulse's stare. He looked reluctant at first, but he nodded his acquiescence. He stepped closer and took Apple's head in his hands. He whispered words into her ear and the girl suddenly went limp, falling into Sabre's waiting arms.

Pulse turned and took Lillith's head in his hands and Elijah tried to shove him away from his wife. Pulse didn't even spare him a passing glance. "You will forget this ever happened," he said into Lillith's ear.

The woman went limp and Pulse gently lowered her to the wooden floor of the porch.

Elijah roared, "What have you done to my wife—"

Pulse grabbed the man's head in his hands and repeated his command. The man looked puzzled for a moment, as if he couldn't believe what was happening, and fell hard to the floor next to his wife, unconscious.

Sabre lifted Apple in his arms, looking down at her with emotion-filled eyes. Luna saw the yearning in the depths of his gaze and looked away, embarrassed to have witnessed such raw desire in the eyes of so fierce a warrior.

Pulse easily lifted Lillith and carried her into the house behind Sabre. The two men set their burdens down on the couch, side by side, and Pulse left once more to retrieve Elijah. He carried the heavy man with little effort, setting him down in the well-worn armchair he'd sat in earlier.

"We must post guards here, to prevent another attack," Pulse said.

Sabre nodded. "I will see to it personally."

Luna was afraid that he would, afraid because the girl was so young, so powerful. But she wisely held her tongue. She knew better than to come between a Shikar and something he wanted. And it was plain to see that Sabre wanted Apple.

"And there must be a cleanup crew to take care of all traces left behind, soon, before this debacle draws any notice," Sabre continued.

Pulse eyed Apple's limp form curiously. "She called stones from the sky."

Luna nodded. "They just came out of nowhere. I've never seen anything like it."

"She is undoubtedly quite powerful," he murmured. "You were wise to lead us here, love."

Luna glowed under his compliment. "Thank you for helping me," she said. "You managed to change things once again."

"We did it together." Pulse reached for her, tucking her beneath his arm. "We must go now, Sabre."

The Shikar nodded and reluctantly looked away from Apple once again. He approached Luna and Pulse, reaching out to take their hands. "Let us be off then," he said roughly.

Luna was prepared this time when the world fell away. But nevertheless, it still made her a little woozy.

Chapter Fourteen

🔊

Pulse called a meeting of the Council to discuss the night's events. Luna decided to stay behind in his room, to relax in silence after the ordeal she had endured. Besides, she figured the Council wouldn't like her attending all their meetings.

Luna stretched out on the plush couch and stared off into space. Time passed, but she didn't know how much. It could have been minutes, it could have been hours. She began to doze off—the calm silence lulling her—only to jerk awake roughly when there was a knock at the door. She rose with a heavy sigh and went to greet whoever was there.

When the door opened and revealed Cady, Luna was more than a little surprised at this unexpected visit. "Hello," she said lamely.

Cady grinned. "Can I come in?" she asked with a twinkle in her eyes.

Luna stepped aside and allowed her entry. The woman looked beautiful in her tight black catsuit. Graceful. Cady took in her surroundings, still smiling, and went to claim the couch. "Sit with me," she said, patting the cushion beside her.

"What's going on?" Luna asked, perching next to her.

"I just wanted to get to know you a little better, that's all. I was surprised to see another human down here."

Luna frowned, puzzled at Cady's choice of words.

Cady laughed. "Don't be confused. You see, I used to be a human."

"No way!" Luna gasped.

"Yes, way."

"But then how did you become…"

"A Shikar?" Cady finished. "Well, that's part of the reason I'm here. I'm meddling. Sid is going to *kill* me when he finds out but I just had to talk to you, to hear what Pulse has told you about our kind."

"He told me how you fight for the human race and for the safety of the world. He's explained a little about your Castes, too. It's pretty amazing, the things all of you can do."

Cady played with the thick braid of hair that fell over her shoulder. "He didn't tell you how Shikars can change some — note that I said *some* — humans into Shikars?"

Luna shook her head, bemused as to where Cady was going with this conversation.

Cady snorted. "Men. Will they never learn that we women can be trusted with whole truths, not just halves?"

Luna realized the implications of what the warrior woman was revealing to her and her curiosity soared. "Can you tell me how they can be…changed?"

"Yeah. It's really quite simple. The semen from a Shikar male is poisonous to most women."

Luna gasped, completely floored by the news. So that was why Pulse was so careful not to spend himself inside her body.

"Yeah. It kills them the moment it's introduced into the woman's system. But there are those of us, people like you and me who have extrasensory perceptions, who don't die when Shikar seed enters our bodies. We're powerful enough to fight off death itself. But we must be sure we love the Shikar or things can go awry. Love is the single most powerful thing in existence. Hands down. It makes us strong, makes us weak, makes us whole, makes us all nuts. And it protects us from harm at the hands of our exotic mates," Cady explained, a soft look in her eyes that belied her blithe tone. Clearly this woman cared enough to share this secret with Luna, and Luna was grateful despite her shock.

After a few moments of digesting all this new information, Luna found her voice once more. "How do you change from human to Shikar? I mean, like, what happens, exactly?" Luna asked.

Cady slung her braid back behind her and sighed. "Our souls travel to the world between this one and death. When we are called back to our bodies by a Traveler, or a strong mate with the ability to Travel through the worlds, we come back changed, physically and mentally."

"How so?"

"We're stronger, for one thing. And we're faster. We're smarter and much more dangerous to our enemies. We are impervious to disease and we heal rapidly, especially when a Shikar with a knack for healing aids us. We take on Caste traits, but there's no rhyme or reason as to what we become. We don't always follow in the footsteps of our mates. For example, I am a Hunter and an Incinerator. Sid, my husband Obsidian, is a multiple Caste too, but different Castes than me. He's a Hunter, a Foil Master and a Traveler. And a fierce warrior too, I'm very proud to say." Cady grinned.

"And Sid changed you?" Luna fairly reeled. The Shikar world, she knew, would always hold surprises for her.

Cady nodded. "We'd only been together a few days. I didn't know about the semen thing. I swallowed some and almost died, but I was saved and when I awoke I was a Shikar. I was the first human to go through the change. But now there's a handful among us. And if things continue as they have, I'm certain there will be many more."

"And you can do anything a Shikar-born person can do?"

"Yeah. Oh—and when we produce children they are exponentially stronger than most Shikars their age. It seems that human genes, however few, when introduced into the Shikar bloodline, results in super-strong babies."

"That's…amazing." Luna was at a loss for words. Why hadn't Pulse told her about this? He should have, if only to warn her away from his semen To explain why he so adamantly strove not to come inside her. Didn't he care enough about her to share the information?

Perhaps it was a well-kept secret. Perhaps Pulse was afraid she'd turn from him, knowing how dangerous he could be for her.

Still, Pulse had told her much about his people. *He should have told me about this, given some hint*, she thought mutinously. He should have trusted her with the knowledge. She'd given him no reason to distrust her.

"I can tell by the look on your face that you're not happy with this news. Might I hazard a guess that it's because you think Pulse should have told you, not me?"

"He should have said *something*." Luna swallowed hard around a sudden aching lump in her throat.

"Well, let me give you some advice. Cut Pulse some slack if you can. All the warriors here are the same. If they think they're protecting us by withholding information, they will do so in a second. They're arrogant, pigheaded, stubborn as all get-out and tight-lipped when it comes to anything related to being a Shikar. I'm sure that eventually

Pulse would have told you himself. But I could see in your eyes that you loved him. I came tonight because I wanted you to know that you have options, should you choose to take advantage of them."

"Thank you," Luna said hoarsely.

Cady laughed, the sound free and full of life. "You can yell at me if you want. I'm meddling where I don't belong and I know it. But I feel a kinship with you—because you're human, because you're powerful, because you're quite obviously a strong and independent woman, whatever— and I wanted to share this with you soon so that you could make an informed decision when the time comes. And trust me," Cady added sagely, "the time will come."

"I don't want to yell at you," Luna said faintly.

"You should. If only to get a little angst off your chest before Pulse comes back and you have a spectacular fight. And believe me, when we fight with our mates it's an awesome sight to behold. I didn't tell you this to make you mad at Pulse, or to make you sad that he didn't tell you himself. I love being a Shikar. But I wasn't given a choice. It's true that we are superior to humans in almost every way, but there are many things about being human that I miss."

"Like what." Luna couldn't imagine Cady as anything but a Shikar.

"Like hotdogs and late-night movies. Like cars and jeans and Godiva chocolates. Like the anonymity of being only one of millions of others just like you. You never realize, until you give it all up, that being a human isn't so bad a thing all the time. Don't get me wrong. I wouldn't trade being a Shikar for all the chocolates in the world. But you still deserve to make your own decision, I think, and to do that you need to know what your options are."

"Thank you for telling me," Luna said softly. "Really. I mean it."

"To counter what I've just said, let me say that being a Shikar is better than anything else in the world. Here there is no need for wealth, no need for greed. Everyone is judged by the strength of their character, not by what brand of clothes they wear. Everyone here is close in some way, and whenever any of us need help there are dozens of loyal hearts ready to be at your back. There are plenty of creature comforts, as I'm sure you've already noticed. And everyone is needed in some way. There are no deadbeats here. Nor are there any Shikars down on their luck or poverty-stricken. We take care of our own no matter what."

"What about freedom?" Luna had been wondering about this from the first moment she'd arrived. "Do you have freedom to be yourself?"

Cady's eyes widened. "*Of course*. I'm no different now than I was when I was human. And though a mate can be very overbearing sometimes, they mean well and would do anything for us. We can come and go as we please down here—for example, you don't have to go out on the battlefield if you don't want to. However, there are always rules on how to conduct oneself up on the surface. It's necessary, to preserve our secrecy. But it's a good trade-off, trust me."

"Do I have to have a mate to stay here?" Luna asked.

Cady eyed her knowingly. "Pulse would say yes, I hazard to guess." She chuckled and patted Luna's leg amiably. "But no, you don't have to be mated. So long as you are happy here and do your part—in your case that means telling the Council when you have a premonition that concerns us—you'll always be welcome here and treated with utmost respect."

Luna took in everything Cady was saying and tried not to be hurt that Pulse had kept these things a secret from her. But then, she couldn't blame him. Not entirely. She knew that she was going to die soon, and so did Pulse. Perhaps he had only been protecting his heart, knowing that he would lose her in the end.

She looked at Cady, meeting the woman's Shikar yellow eyes for a long moment. "Your son is going to set fire to your living room tomorrow morning," she said softly.

"*What*?" Cady started. "You know that?"

"Yes. He'll injure his babysitter—she'll contract some third-degree burns."

"Then I shall ensure that I'm with him at all times tomorrow and give the babysitter the day off. I only need a couple hours of sleep anyway." She laughed, a full-throated sound, and smiled wryly. There was great dawning admiration in her eyes, which made Luna feel a little uncomfortable, but warm and fuzzy all the same. "Thank you for warning me."

"Thank you for coming here tonight."

"You don't have to thank me. I know my news doesn't sit well with you. And how could it? This changes things, doesn't it?"

"Yes," Luna agreed.

"Just remember that you are among friends here. If you need any help, anything at all, just let us know. And whether you choose to become a Shikar or not is between you and Pulse. Whatever choice you make together will be the right one."

Luna nodded.

"Well…" Cady bounded to her feet. "I'd better leave before Sid comes looking for me. I kinda left him in a tizzy. He's still pissed that I let Daemon go."

"Daemon? You mean the monsters?" Luna frowned. "Why would you do that?"

Cady shook her head and made for the door. "No. *Daemon* is the Lord of the Horde. He's the creator of the monsters we fight. But he didn't mean for things to get this bad. He didn't originally create the Daemons to bedevil us. He's really not a bad guy, even if he is a dark motherfucker. He saved my brother's life, and for that alone I'd brave my husband's anger in setting him free. And even though Sid secretly admires what I did—yeah, I can tell that easily enough—he still has to pretend to be a little angry for a while yet."

With that the vivacious woman cast a small, gentle smile over her shoulder at Luna, who followed her to the door. "Don't worry, Luna. Everything will work out. I don't have to be clairvoyant to know that."

Luna watched Cady's retreating back until she lost sight of her in the distance. Letting out a huge sigh, she closed the door and went back into the sitting room, waiting for Pulse to return to her.

* * * * *

Pulse watched as his fellow Council members filed out of the meeting hall. The meeting had gone well. Everyone was pleased to know that the Daemon attack had been thwarted and a powerful human had been saved. Sabre assigned warriors to watch over Apple at all hours of the night, to ensure that she was kept safe. Everyone had been grateful to Luna for her warning and courage in the face of danger.

Pulse had never been so proud. His woman was a surprise to everyone, including himself. She never wavered in her purpose, not even when facing their worst enemies. She was so brave, wanting to make a difference in everyone's lives. And though she'd lived a harsh life herself, she still managed to see the beauty in the world around her.

He loved her, he realized. He had loved her since seeing her step in front of a taxicab in order to save a woman's—a stranger's—life. His fate had been sealed the moment he'd met her.

But he needed to tell her, and tell her the right way. Tell her that he loved her more than the air he breathed. Tell her that he treasured her love in return as he had treasured nothing else in his life. And tell her that they could be together, forever, if she desired it.

He refused to think about her dying. She may have known the how and part of the when, but he vowed he would not let her go into death's waiting embrace alone. He couldn't live without her. It was as simple as that. He must find a way to save her from her fate, and soon. For now, he vowed to keep her warm and away from cold climes.

In the meantime he would ask that she share her life with him. He would tell her how she could be his mate forever. He would give her the choice of becoming like him. A Shikar.

He hurried home, eager to be with her. He had missed her for the past two hours during his Council session. He wanted her at his side. Always. Being separated from her, even for a couple hours, was sheer torture. He wanted her in sight, within arm's reach at all times. He wondered how she'd feel about that and smiled. His woman was a firecracker. There was no telling how she would react to his newfound addiction to her nearness.

He wondered what kind of Shikar she would make. There was no way to determine what Caste she would be. And there was every possibility that her powers would multiply exponentially—he didn't know how she'd feel about that, either. Her premonitions were already a burden as they were now.

There was a chance that she would not choose the path of a Shikar. He had to prepare himself for that possibility, though it hurt to even think about it. She was a strong-willed woman, and she might treasure her humanity above all else. He hoped not. He knew that turning her would be difficult and fraught with danger, but he also knew that she would make a splendid Shikar in the end, if only she wanted to.

He hoped that she was ready to make the choice. Because he already had. And for him there was no turning back.

Chapter Fifteen

ဢ

Luna started when the door to the apartment opened and Pulse stepped in. She had been waiting in the silence, thoughts racing, doubts abounding. Everything Cady said went through her mind over and over, torturing her. Why hadn't he told her? That was the biggest question of all and she had no guess as to the answer.

Pulse came to the couch where she sat and leaned down to kiss her warmly on the mouth. He pulled back and settled onto the cushion next to her, putting his arm around her shoulders. "I missed you," he said softly in her ear, his breath tickling the hairs at the nape of her neck.

Luna didn't know how to be diplomatic so she didn't even try. "Do you love me, Pulse?" she asked tremulously.

Pulse started. "I do," he said after a beat. "I am shamed to admit that I've only just realized it—so much has happened in so short a time—but I do love you. Very much. More than anyone could ever love another."

"Why didn't you tell me that I could become a Shikar like you?"

Pulse sighed and pulled his arm back, threading his fingers together in his lap. He met her gaze with his and some of the fear and doubt left her. "I was not ready to go down that road yet, I suppose. I had thought of it—of course I had—but I was afraid what you would think if I told you. I thought you might get scared of making love with me."

Luna smiled. "Nothing could keep me from making love with you."

"Who told you about this?" he asked.

"Cady."

Pulse closed his eyes and shook his head. "I should have known. I've heard much about Cady's exploits. It shouldn't surprise me that she felt a kinship with you and thought to prepare you for what may lie ahead. I only wish she had waited a couple more risings before she said anything."

"Were you going to tell me?" she asked softly.

"I was. Tonight. I had decided the moment I left here. Are you angry that I didn't tell you sooner?"

Luna sighed. "Not really. I mean, I was hurt when I thought you had kept it a secret from me. It explained a lot that I was curious about, such as why you wouldn't come inside me. It also made me question a lot of things."

"Like what?"

"Well, for one, I wondered if you would even want me as a mate. For another, I wondered how I could find the courage to become a Shikar, if given the choice. I've never wanted to be anything more than I am, anything more than human. But I was never just an ordinary human anyway, no matter how hard I tried to pretend sometimes. I wondered if I could give up my old life and assume another one and still be myself. Inside."

Pulse turned and pulled her close and turned them so that they were spooning on the couch. "You'll always be you. Becoming a Shikar won't change that."

"How can you be sure?" she asked.

He thought for a moment. "None of the women who have been changed were altered beyond their physical selves. Their personalities stayed the same. Their hopes and dreams and desires were no different than they had been when they were human. I'm certain that there is no risk of you losing yourself."

"Do you want me as a mate?" she asked tremulously, half dreading, half anticipating his answer.

Pulse clutched her closer and kissed her temple. "I do. I want it more than anything I have ever wanted in my life. You're everything to me. I couldn't live without you by my side. I don't know how I ever did."

"Do you want me to be a Shikar?"

"You are very strong as a human. You will be far stronger as a Shikar. You will live much longer, never have to worry about disease and perhaps even learn to control your clairvoyant abilities. Do *you* want to be a Shikar?"

Luna relaxed against him. "If I become a Shikar there are going to have to be conditions," she said.

"What are they?"

"I don't want to be kept down here like a prisoner. I want to be able to go up to the surface world whenever I want."

Pulse thought quietly for a moment. "I would let you go anytime you wanted so long as I am with you. How is that?"

Luna nodded. "That's cool. I don't like to be away from you either."

"What other conditions do you have?"

"You have to swear to me that you'll never leave me. I don't think I could handle being cast aside."

Pulse laughed, surprising her. "Love, no warrior that I know has mated only to change their minds afterward. We seem to mate for life, once we find the right woman to love. Love is our true strength and our very lifeblood."

"Promise me you won't dump me."

"I won't 'dump' you. I promise." He laughed softly.

Luna let out a sigh of relief. "I'm sorry. I just had to know you weren't going to get tired of me."

"I won't. How could I ever? You're a walking surprise from the moment you wake to the moment you sleep. You will always keep me on my toes. I only worry that you will tire of *me*. I can be…overbearing at times."

Luna laughed. "At times? You mean all the time, don't you?"

He tickled her sides, making her giggle and squirm in his embrace. "So what if I am? You like me that way."

"I guess I do." She laughed again and swatted his roaming hands away. She sobered. "But there is one little problem."

"What's that?" he asked, concerned.

"I'm going to die, Pulse," she said quietly. "Soon. I know it. I have seen it."

"You will never freeze down here," he said fiercely. "I will keep you warm, always."

Luna took a deep, calming breath and swallowed around the lump in her throat. Pulse may have been confident that he could keep her from dying, but she was quite a lot more skeptical. "You can't change fate," she said at last.

"How can you say that? After everything I have done and been through together? Haven't you learned yet that we are an unstoppable team, you and I? Together we can change anything we wish—including fate." He kissed the top of her head. "You shouldn't worry so, love."

"I can't help it. Since I met you, I've felt the weight of my death bearing down upon me. Before I met you, I didn't really care that I would die. Now I want to live."

"And you will," Pulse said. He rose and bent over her, scooping her up into his arms. He turned and carried her to the bedroom. "We'll make certain of it. Together."

Luna put her arms around his neck and hugged him tight. He deposited her lightly onto the bed and came down to join her. They reclined on their sides, regarding each other intently.

"Do you want to become a Shikar?" he asked.

Luna thought, searching deep inside herself for the truth, just to be sure, and finally nodded, knowing it was the right choice. She really did want to be like him. Strong like him, smart and sure like him.

"Do you want to become one tonight?" he murmured softly.

Luna nodded. "Okay." She grinned then and felt her nipples harden to almost painful points of desire.

"I have obviously never done this before, so I can't tell you exactly what to expect. Just remember that I love you and I won't let you go into the unknown alone."

Luna reached for him and silenced him with a kiss. "I trust you," she whispered against his lips.

Pulse grabbed her head and pulled her closer, slanting his mouth over hers, delving his tongue deep into her secrets. His tongue was hot and smooth and wet, touching and tasting every inch of her mouth. She suckled on his tongue, wringing a groan from his lips that sent her heart racing.

His hands found the hem of her T-shirt and pulled it up and off slowly. Finding the front clasp of her bra, he flicked it open with his fingers and it fell away, revealing all her naked skin to his hot, hungry gaze.

He bent to her once more and nibbled lightly on her lips, breathing softly into her mouth. His fingers trailed down her cheeks and throat. One hand cupped her neck gently while the other sought out her aching breast. Luna arched into his touch, her thick, erect nipple stabbing into his palm demandingly.

The rough pads of his fingers twisted her nipple gently and his hand hefted the weight of her breast, cupping it tenderly. His lips trailed down to her chin, throat and shoulder, burning her flesh in their wake. He ran his tongue over her shoulder and blew lightly on the wetness he left behind, cooling the fire he had stoked. Her skin broke out in goose pimples and she shivered in his embrace, moaning softly.

Pulse ran his hands all over her torso, until she was gasping for breath and arching uncontrollably into his touch. His deft fingers undid the button and zipper of her jeans. He pushed them down her hips and pulled them off. All that kept him from gazing on her full nudity was a scrap of silk panties, which he tore in his haste to remove, his roughness enflaming both their senses.

He left her and removed his own clothes with a speed that surprised her. The bright glow of his eyes burned a trail from the top of her head to the tips of her toes, lingering on her breasts, belly, cunt and legs. Pulse fell on her again, growling like a ravenous beast, taking her nipple deep into his mouth and suckling it until she cried out and clutched him to her.

When their skin met it was as though a lightning bolt had shot through them, and the smell of ozone was thick in the air. He trailed his fingers down her stomach, shocking her, sparks flying, blinding her. Every hair on her body stood at attention, and the feel of his power humming through her made her breath come in short, desperate gasps.

Her head thrashed on the pillow as he moved from one nipple to the other, teasing and tormenting her to the point of madness. His hair fell over them like a black veil, the silver strands twinkling like stars shining in a blanket of night. His scent, woodsy and wild and totally male, teased her senses, flooding through her until she couldn't take a breath that didn't smell and taste of him.

The storm of need that rode her raged to new heights. She pushed him back forcefully and came over him. She let her hair and her lips trail lightly over the thick muscles of his chest, on to his rippling belly and lower.

When she took him into her mouth, Pulse roared and fisted his hands in her hair. The plum-shaped head of his erection slipped between her lips and she licked the crown, flicking her tongue over the sensitive flesh. His hips bucked up and pushed his cock deeper into her mouth and she took him until he touched the back of her throat.

Running her tongue along the length and breadth of him, she bobbed her head up and down on his shaft, sucking his cock until she was dizzy with desire. His flavor was wild on her tongue, intoxicating. Addicting. He was like velvet-covered steel in her mouth, stretching her lips wide around his great girth.

With a growl, Pulse pulled her off him and turned her so that she was on her hands and knees in front of him. He came up behind her and felt her wetness with the tips of his fingers. He grabbed the thick base of his cock in his hand and guided it into her hot, welcoming body. The crown slipped into her with a popping sensation, and then he stretched her impossibly tight as he filled her inch by delicious inch.

Luna arched back into him, swallowing his cock with her hungry pussy. Her clit swelled and ached, and it seemed that Pulse knew what she needed. One hand came around her, the other holding tight to her hip, and zeroed in on her pulsing nubbin of flesh. He rubbed tight little circles into her, making stars burst behind her eyes.

She bent lower, raising her hips to take him deeper. He filled her so completely that she didn't know where she stopped and he began. Her heart thundered in her breast and her senses reeled. Lust, need and love swamped her, making her motions more frantic, more hungry.

Her climax surprised her. She came with a short scream, feeling her pussy milk his cock demandingly. Tremors shook her from within and she felt a gush of wetness wash around his erection, making him slip and slide into her even more easily.

When she came down, he was there to push her right back up. His fingers concentrated on her clit, rubbing it, squeezing it, pressing in upon it. Luna arched back, feeling him slam into her body, keening high in the back of her throat as another climax raged through her.

He rode her hard. Though his hands were tender they were also demanding, driving her up to yet another peak. His sac slapped gently against her with each downward stroke, and the wet, sucking sounds their bodies made enflamed them both into mindless desire.

"I'm going to come," he rasped, pounding into her, letting her come down from her high gently. "Stay with me, Luna. Do not go into the darkness alone."

He hammered his cock into her cunt. He felt so good inside her that tears streamed from her eyes. Her heart swelled painfully in her breast and her breath came hard into her lungs. She'd never been so aroused.

With one last mighty plunge, he shouted and spurted his cum deep inside her. Luna felt the hot splash of his seed burning her insides, filling her up, overflowing between their bodies.

He shuddered over her and withdrew himself from her body. He turned them so that they both lay on their sides, spooning, with him in back. Luna caught her breath and let the last of her climactic tremors lull her into a pool of relaxation.

Cold shot through her and she gasped, shooting up in the bed. It felt as though her blood had turned to ice in her veins and was pumping frost throughout her form. Her body shivered and every muscle tightened most painfully, causing her to cry out and thrash back against the pillows.

Pulse's arms came around her but she did not feel their warmth. It was as if she would never feel warmth again. Her teeth chattered and her breath shuddered in and out of her frozen lungs.

"I'm dying," she managed to whisper, her tone filled with a strange mix of awe and disappointment, before thrashing back against him uncontrollably.

"It's okay. I won't let you go," he promised, a catch in his voice. "I've got you."

"I'm freezing. I'm going to die." Tears poured from her eyes, but they too felt cold.

"No, you're not," he said vehemently.

Blackness flooded over her, through her, and Pulse's voice faded away. She was so scared. She knew this was it—this was the death she had foreseen for herself. Her only regret was that she was leaving Pulse behind alone. Dying in his arms was really going to mess with him, she knew.

What a pisser.

188

She let the darkness take her, felt her soul leaving her body behind, with all its aches and pains and pleasures. The gaping maw of a great void loomed ahead of her, beckoning to her. It felt as though she were flying through space, racing to the world that she felt sure lay beyond this one. But she lingered. Something was holding her back.

"Come back to me," she heard a voice say in the dark. She felt the sheltering warmth of power flood through her and she realized that Pulse was here with her in this nothingness. She tried to call to him, but she had no voice with which to speak.

She moved inexorably closer to the void. Pulse held her back and it felt as if his arms were cradling her. Some of the cold left her and she tried to turn back to her lover, but it was almost impossible. The next world beckoned demandingly.

"No. You're coming back, Luna. Don't let go," Pulse begged, and the words echoed in her ears as if he were right there beside her.

Luna felt her soul get sucked backward, a dizzying rush of space flying by. With a sickening jolt her soul returned to her body, jarring her. With a short, broken scream she reared up and found herself sitting on the floor in Pulse's arms. "What happened?" she asked weakly, trembling violently from head to toe. "Why am I not dead?" Her mouth was dry, her voice rough and gravelly as if she'd been screaming.

The splash of a hot tear hit her cheek and she realized Pulse was weeping as he cradled her close. "You're a Shikar now," he said softly, rubbing his hands down her back in a soothing motion. Luna leaned back, weary and sore, and caught the tears that fell from his eyes with her shaking fingers, brushing them away. "You're my mate in every way," he whispered. "Mine and mine alone."

Luna felt a sharp pain lance through her head and she gasped, jerking back reflexively, putting her hand to her head. "Ahhh," she moaned. Another pain hit her and she pulled from Pulse's embrace, staggering to her feet. Pulse rose with her, hands out in case she should fall, and watched her with concern.

"What is it?" he asked.

Luna shuddered then felt her body snap into an almost trancelike stillness. "There will be a flood in Kansas two days from now." She pressed her palms on either side of her head, as if she could squeeze the premonition out forcibly. "Nancy Carte of Seattle will die in an office fire."

Pulse took hold of her gently, breathing raggedly, concern transforming his features to stone.

"Don't let Flare go to the Territories next Friday. There will be an ambush waiting for him on the outskirts of Paris. He'll be hurt pretty badly."

"I won't," he agreed reverently, holding her more and more tightly. "I'll transfer him to Germany or Russia for a couple weeks."

"I can see so many things," she cried, seeing not the room before her but a thousand visions, one after the other, a sea of knowledge that threatened to drive her mad. She shrieked, clutching desperately at her head which felt full to bursting, and jerked in the arms of her love. "Your niece will Travel with your spies tomorrow night and find her mate among the humans of San Francisco."

Pulse started. "Luna! By Grimm, Luna, that wasn't a bad prediction! You realize what this means?"

She shook her head then gagged as the motion made her dizzy. "Mike Hamil of northern Kentucky will win the Indiana Powerball lottery." The words spilled from her mouth uncontrollably, so fast they hummed.

"You're making predictions of things that are positive," he said with a grin full of relief, full of joy. "Try to push them back, deep into the back of your mind. Concentrate." He soothed her, repeating the words over and over like a mantra, knowing in his heart that all would be well.

Luna tried to find an anchor in the chaos and found it in Pulse's arms. "There will be a prison break in Cornelia, Georgia. Two men will be caught but the third will get away for two weeks and father a child with his longtime girlfriend. The baby will be a girl."

"Try to control it, Luna. You must try. You won't be able to go on like this." Concern was writ plainly on his handsome features and in his tone, but the love and joy shone through despite it all.

She shuddered in his arms and squeezed her eyes tightly shut. So many premonitions flooded through her that she felt she might burst open, like a dam that has been broken. She knew so much, so fast, that her mind reeled. Luna held her breath and focused on pushing the images aside, painstakingly building an imaginary wall between them and the rest of her brain.

Several minutes passed as she recovered her breath and the racing of her heart gentled. "I think...god, I think they've passed now," she managed tremulously, still shivering uncontrollably despite her best efforts to remain still.

"Your powers have increased exponentially. I've never witnessed anything like this," Pulse said, clutching her tight.

"I see everything," she said with a whimper. "I know everything."

"Can you keep the premonitions at bay? Can you control them?"

She swallowed hard, throat parched, and nodded. "I think so. Eventually, anyway. Maybe. I don't know." She rambled the words so quickly they sounded like one long word.

"You are truly a miracle," he told her, tender, reverent awe in his voice.

Luna shook her head. "No, I'm not. *You* are. You kept me from dying, bringing me back to life, bringing me back to you."

"We did it together."

"Yes. Together. And we'll always be together now," she murmured, resting her forehead on his chest wearily. "Won't we?"

"Forever. In this life and the one beyond," he vowed.

She sighed heavily. "God, I'm so sore. It feels like I've gone five rounds with George Foreman."

"Come back to bed with me. You need your rest." He pulled her to the bed, lowering her onto it slowly, gently.

"Cady's pregnant. Her child will be a Traveler," she whispered faintly. "A really, really strong warrior."

"That's enough now. Let it all go. Don't think about anything," Pulse instructed softly.

Luna shivered, teeth chattering, and immediately fell into a deep, exhausted sleep where, blessedly, the visions left her in peace.

Epilogue

ॐ

"I'm pregnant."

Pulse looked up from the ledger he had been studying. The paper was more beige than yellow, giving it an old look though it was new. Shikar paper was made from something other than trees. Luna didn't know what it was made of, she just knew its production was less destructive to the environment than that of the paper she was used to.

"What did you say?" he asked hoarsely.

Luna smiled at his bewildered look. "I'm pregnant. With triplets. Two girls and a boy."

"You are certain?" He was quite obviously dumbfounded.

"Yes. And I have a strong feeling that all three of them will be able to control lightning, as you do." She patted her tummy lovingly.

Pulse looked at her, wide-eyed. Then he bounded from his chair and grabbed her, swinging her around in a circle, laughing joyously, whooping and shouting. "This is incredible news!" He put her down. "I have to tell everyone," he said, racing for the door.

Luna laughed and ran after him. "Come back. Let's just keep it between us for a few days, huh?"

Pulse stopped just steps outside the apartment. "Why? Is something wrong?"

Luna knew he was going to be a bear during this pregnancy. He worried far too much, even on the most benign of days. "No, nothing's wrong. I just want to savor the news together for a while. You know, try on the parental shoes and stuff. Try to imagine what our lives will be like in nine months or so."

He jerked her up into his arms and kissed her hard. He set her back just as quickly, making her dizzy. "I love you," he said, touching her stomach reverently. "You've made me the happiest being alive. I can't wait until we have a family—do you know what they'll look like?"

Luna shook her head. "No. But I know they'll be healthy. And the delivery will be surprisingly hassle-free, thank friggin' goodness. I'll deliver them in our own bed, our own bedroom—what do you think?"

"I think it's an excellent notion." He kissed her again and this time he lingered.

Pulse lifted her in his arms and carried her back into their home, kicking the door closed behind them. He lowered her to the floor before pressing her against the door and undressing her with quick, eager hands. When she was nude he turned his attention to his own clothes, ripping them off his body hastily. He came back to her, pressing his hot, naked skin to hers, warming her from head to toe.

He lifted her off her feet and she wound her legs around his waist. Pulse rubbed his cock into the wet heat of her pussy and groaned. He moved his hips and thrust into her hard, jarring her to the back of her teeth. Luna cried out and clutched him to her, letting him bounce her upon him, entering her over and over again.

"I love you so much, Luna. My form is filled with it, with you. I will always love you," he gasped, taking her mouth roughly.

Luna moaned and let her head fall back, opening her lips to allow entrance to his tongue. His pelvis ground against hers, causing enough friction against her clit to make her tremble uncontrollably in his embrace. His cock hit some magical spot deep within her body, making her see stars, the pleasure was so immediate and intense.

"I've never needed anyone the way I need you," he said roughly.

"Oh, Pulse, that feels *sooo* good," she groaned.

"Come for me, love. Let me feel your sweet pussy swallow my cock."

He brushed that magical place inside her and she flew straight into climax. Pulse thrust into her harder, faster, and joined her only seconds later.

As they came, they held each other tight, riding out the storm together. And Luna knew, without a doubt, that everything in her life was going to be okay. She didn't need a premonition to tell her—she just knew it. Collapsing against him she realized she had come this far, for so long, with only one purpose. To love him. To be loved by him. Forever.

"I love you, Pulse," she whispered.

"I love you, too, Luna. Forever."

Forever. Now she could get used to that idea.

But she wondered…how would he react when she told him… Ah hell, who cared?

He loved her, she loved him and love always made everything all right. No matter how crazy the world could be.

Enjoy an excerpt from:
CARESS OF FLAME

When it was her turn to go out onto the stage, Isis almost froze. That feeling of being watched, of being the subject of a very hungry gaze, had come back with brute force. She was nearly immobilized by fear for a few long seconds and then Isis forced herself to pass the curtain and enter the stage, still breathless with worry.

Of course someone was watching her, Isis chided herself. She was a stripper. Dozens of eyes watched her every night. With this reminder, she threw herself into her routine.

She skipped to the center of the stage to give her virginal look a more authentic feel for her audience. However, she shattered that illusion when she did a slow back flip, revealing her crotch to the crowd, and skillfully unzipped the back of her dress.

Her virginal attire slipped unheeded to the floor. She danced, undulating her hips suggestively, letting her breasts bob with each movement, and casually unhooked the front clasp of her bra. Isis then made a great show of taking off her bra, throwing it into the crowd. Money waved wildly about the stage and Isis bent to let several men stuff bills into her panties. She saw even more waving and knew that tonight she'd make a lot of money.

What she didn't see was the six and a half foot, two hundred and fifty pounds of muscle marching up to the stage. She finally saw him when the dark man shoved some of her customers to the side and approached her, climbing onto the stage.

Isis backed up, knowing the bouncers behind her were coming forward to escort the giant off the stage. But her eyes never left his—they were pale yellow with an orange fire in the center. They burned right through her, as if he could see into her soul. His hair caught her eye then—it was so long and so straight. It shone like a mirror and was so black as to be almost blue in the bright lights of the stage.

Jack, the first bouncer to reach the dark man, put his arm out to stop him from getting any closer to Isis. With one well-practiced move the dark man grabbed Jack's hand and karate chopped his arm. Isis, as well as everyone else around the stage, heard the sound of Jack's arm breaking, even over the loud music still playing. The dark man shoved Jack off the stage and into the crowd.

Shrieks sounded out and the music stopped. The lights came up in the club, blinding everyone for a second except for Isis, who was still framed by the spotlight. She stood frozen, unable to move. As if watching a play she stared, dazed, as the second bouncer, Mike, came forward and made a grab for the dark man. The dark man felled the bouncer with nothing but a punch to his jaw. Mike went down hard and the man advanced.

Isis' paralysis broke and she turned to run. Something hit her with the force of a battering ram. She was spun around by hands stronger than any human's she'd ever come across and thrown roughly, unceremoniously over the dark man's shoulder. In a growing panic Isis beat at his back and buttocks, unavoidably noticing how hard and muscular the giant was.

Another bouncer had reached them. The dark man grabbed the bouncer by the neck and, with an almost casual flick of his wrist, threw him several feet across the room, tables and chairs spilling as the bouncer landed. Hard.

Isis roared and sank her teeth into the lower back of her captor, gagging as the dark man's hair filled her mouth along with his flesh. The man didn't even flinch.

Chaos ruled the club. People everywhere were running for the exits. Another bouncer carefully approached them. Isis could see him out of the corner of her eye. She continued to pummel the dark man, but none of her blows seemed to even faze him as he let the bouncers get closer.

She rose up, putting her hands on the dark man's back so that she could look over his shoulder. What she saw froze her heart with fear.

The dark man raised his hand, palm out, and pulled it back as if he were about to pitch a baseball—then an incredibly hot burst of air exploded out of his hand and sent the bouncer flying backward, helpless. Isis felt the heat of that strange wind and she knew immediately that this was the man she'd seen the night before. She remembered that heart exploding into fire in the dark man's palm and at once knew a true, very elemental fear.

Isis bucked wildly, trying to dislodge herself. The man put his hand on her ass—his skin was so *hot*—and effectively stilled her panicked movements. More bouncers approached, but none were foolish enough to get too close to the man who held her captive. Soon all the bouncers who worked in the club surrounded them and Isis felt sure that, with their combined strength, they could free her from this frightening man.

The world fell away and Isis screamed as the sensation of incredible speed overcame her. The G-force pressed her legs against the man's muscular chest. He still hadn't taken his hand from her ass and for some reason that was the most noticeable thing in the strange nothingness Isis found herself flying through. She felt a sick clenching of her stomach and the next thing she knew they were standing in a room she'd never seen before.

Isis was unceremoniously thrown onto the softest, largest bed she'd ever seen. An article of clothing was tossed in her face.

"I'll leave while you dress," the man said in a voice that made her instantly wet. She tamped down on her very unexpected spurt of desire, reminding herself of what this man could do to her if he so chose. Without another word, the dark man turned and left the room, audibly locking the door behind him.

Why an electronic book?

We live in the Information Age — an exciting time in the history of human civilization, in which technology rules supreme and continues to progress in leaps and bounds every minute of every day. For a multitude of reasons, more and more avid literary fans are opting to purchase e-books instead of paper books. The question from those not yet initiated into the world of electronic reading is simply: *Why?*

1. ***Price.*** An electronic title at Ellora's Cave Publishing and Cerridwen Press runs anywhere from 40% to 75% less than the cover price of the exact same title in paperback format. Why? Basic mathematics and cost. It is less expensive to publish an e-book (no paper and printing, no warehousing and shipping) than it is to publish a paperback, so the savings are passed along to the consumer.

2. ***Space.*** Running out of room in your house for your books? That is one worry you will never have with electronic books. For a low one-time cost, you can purchase a handheld device specifically designed for e-reading. Many e-readers have large, convenient screens for viewing. Better yet, hundreds of titles can be stored within your new library — on a single microchip. There are a variety of e-readers from different manufacturers. You can also read e-books on your PC or laptop computer. (Please note that Ellora's Cave does not endorse any specific brands. You can check our websites at www.ellorascave.com

or www.cerridwenpress.com for information we make available to new consumers.)

3. *Mobility.* Because your new e-library consists of only a microchip within a small, easily transportable e-reader, your entire cache of books can be taken with you wherever you go.

4. *Personal Viewing Preferences.* Are the words you are currently reading too small? Too large? Too... ANNOYING? Paperback books cannot be modified according to personal preferences, but e-books can.

5. *Instant Gratification.* Is it the middle of the night and all the bookstores near you are closed? Are you tired of waiting days, sometimes weeks, for bookstores to ship the novels you bought? Ellora's Cave Publishing sells instantaneous downloads twenty-four hours a day, seven days a week, every day of the year. Our webstore is never closed. Our e-book delivery system is 100% automated, meaning your order is filled as soon as you pay for it.

Those are a few of the top reasons why electronic books are replacing paperbacks for many avid readers.

As always, Ellora's Cave and Cerridwen Press welcome your questions and comments. We invite you to email us at Comments@ellorascave.com or write to us directly at Ellora's Cave Publishing Inc., 1056 Home Avenue, Akron, OH 44310-3502.

MAKE EACH DAY MORE *EXCITING* WITH OUR

ELLORA'S
CAVEMEN
CALENDAR

WWW.ELLORASCAVE.COM